Frederick Germaine
Presents

Ladies' Man 2
An Entertaining Love Novel

Copyright © 2014 by Frederick Germaine
Published by: F. Germaine Publishing
Cover Design: Brand Concepts Creative Media
ISBN: 978-0-692-22351-2

Printed in the United States of America.

Dedication:

This is dedicated to all the fans from the ATL to Australia and every point in between. Without you I am absolutely positively nothing. Continue to love me because I love you.

LADIES' MAN 2

AN ENTERTAINING LOVE NOVEL

F. GERMAINE PUBLISHING
ATLANTA, GEORGIA

WWW.FREDERICKGERMAINE.COM

PART I

A NEW BEGINNING

SPRING 2009

CHAPTER 1

It was a Thursday afternoon and I arrived at the Ritz-Carlton Hotel on Peachtree Road in Buckhead. Even though I second-guessed my decision, I was there to meet with Nicole. She was more than anxious to help me get my new consulting business off the ground. More than that, I taken it upon myself to forgive her for all the shenanigans she put me through.

"Hello, sir," said the amicable woman as I walked up to the front desk. "Will you need a room this afternoon or do you have reservations?"

"Actually, I'm here to meet someone," I replied as I looked around the stylish lobby. "I was supposed to meet her in the lobby but I don't see her anywhere."

"Well, I should be able to assist you," said the front desk attendant remaining cheerful. "What's the name of the person you're supposed to be meeting with?"

"Her name is Nicole Jones," I reluctantly answered.

"Oh, Mrs. Jones is a regular guest here. May I have your name, sir?"

"Yes, it's Damien Hardy."

The friendly woman looked down for a second and quickly typed on the keyboard to the computer in front of her. Then she reached into a drawer, near her, and pulled out an object that resembled a credit card.

"Mrs. Jones requested you meet with her in room 1902," said the woman smiling.

"In her room," I said looking astonished. "Are you sure?"

"Yes, sir, I'm quite sure," she replied handing me the slim object. "Per Mrs. Jones' request, here is a complimentary key to her room. You'll find the elevators down the hall to your left."

"Okay," I said as I grabbed the card key from her.

"Enjoy your stay, sir," said the woman before I departed.

"Thank you," I responded as I headed towards the elevators.

As I walked vigorously down the hall, I promised myself there wasn't going to be any sex between Nicole and me. The meeting between us was strictly business and I planned to keep it that way.

When I arrived at the elevators, lucky for me, the door opened up. I quickly hopped inside the well-lit confines of the small space. Then I pressed the button to the nineteenth floor. While moving upwards at a rapid speed, I contemplated whether or not I was doing the right thing. I looked at the door key in my hand and then back to the numbers on the elevator's control panel. Maybe meeting with Nicole at the Ritz-Carlton Hotel was the wrong move, so I inched my hand to press the button for the lobby. As my hand moved forward, there was soft chime letting me know I had arrived at my destination. I pulled my hand back, stepped out the elevator, and walked down the narrow isle to Nicole's room.

Standing in front of Nicole's door, I once again looked at the door key in my hand. I assured myself this was a business meeting and if anything was to go awry I would quickly get the hell out of there. Then, I softly knocked on the door not wanting to catch Nicole off guard before entering. After no response, I quickly put the card key into the door slot and removed it. There was a click sound letting me know I had access to the room. So, I entered and closed the door behind me.

4

"What took you so long?" asked Nicole standing a few feet in front of me.

I was speechless and couldn't say a word. The only thing I could think about was how gorgeous Nicole still looked. She was only wearing a black colored laced bra and panties. In her hand was a glass of wine which she rapidly placed to her lips.

"Look, Nicole, maybe this is not such a good idea for us to meet again," I finally answered gathering my thoughts.

"Oh, don't be silly, Damien," she announced after removing the glass from her mouth. Then she moved closer towards me until she was right in my face. "This is only a business meeting, right?"

"It depends on what you're referring to when you say business," I responded looking straight into her eyes.

Nicole looked to her right and decided to put the glass of wine on the counter which was next to us. Then, forcefully she took both of her hands and placed them on my face.

"Oh, baby, it's going to be so good between us better than what it used to be."

"Nicole, I didn't come here for this!"

"But my husband, Maurice, secured another job

making over six figures and I can really help your business succeed."

"I understand, Nicole, but not like this."

She didn't hesitate any longer and began to kiss me frantically. I could tell from the aroma of the wine she had been drinking Chardonnay.

"Baby, I missed you so much," she whispered as I pulled away. "I've been keeping this sweet black pussy real tight for you too. Don't you want some?"

"No, Nicole, I don't." I replied not wholeheartedly telling the truth while reaching for the door. "I think it's best if I leave now."

"Don't go just yet, Damien," Nicole yelled out as she grabbed my hand. Just give me a few seconds because I want to show you something."

"Okay, I'll give you a moment," I said with a serious demeanor looking into her eyes. "But make it snappy because the clock is ticking."

Nicole didn't waste any time and quickly had me follow her. While doing this, she kept a firm grip on my hand leading the way. Now, it's been said plenty of times that a hard dick has no conscious. My heart was telling me to stop but the wrong head was inching me on to go get that sweet black pussy. And watching Nicole's fine ass shake in front of me didn't help the situation at all. Finally, we ended up in the bedroom facing each other. Her bed was directly behind me.

"Now, lie back on the bed, relax, and watch the show," she demanded.

"Alright, whatever you say," I said complying with her demand.

As I lay on the bed fully stretched out, I watched Nicole remove her bra. She placed her luscious breasts in both hands and began to lick them. While doing this, she moaned loudly knowing that would turn me on. Then she took off her panties and slightly spreads open her legs. She began to massage her clit with a few of her fingers moaning even louder. Then she inserted them into her pussy so they would be good and wet. To cap off the sex show, she licked her fingers then jumped on top of me. Slowly, she rubbed those same fingers over my lips and I eagerly opened my mouth.

"Now, baby, doesn't my sweet black pussy still taste good?" she asked.

"As always," I exclaimed eagerly licking the juice from her fingers.

Nicole quickly reached under the over-sized pillow, I was laying on, and pulled out a pair of steel handcuffs.

They were shiny and most importantly real.

"Put your hands behind your head," she ordered.

"Damn, you're still kinky as always," I said while I placed both of my hands behind my head.

"Nicole took the handcuffs and secured my wrists to the bed posts. The she ripped open my shirt, licked my nipples, and moved down my abs. Soon enough, she removed my slacks where my eight-inch rock-hard dick was awaiting her. She placed me into her welcoming warm mouth. The sight of her head bobbing up and down turned me on even more.

"Baby, my wet pussy wants to devour your thick long black dick."

"Then hop your sexy ass on top of it now."

Nicole rode me eloquently as her wet pussy loosened up real quick. Slowly, her pussy fully swallowed my hard dick. Juices flowed down the shaft of my dick as she began to ride me faster. I wanted to spread her ass even more, with my hands, so I could thrust further inside her. But the only thing I could do was yank the handcuffs that weren't bulging from the bed posts. Our lips met as we closed out eyes and began to kiss passionately.

She suddenly stopped kissing me and exited off my hard dick. I opened my eyes wondering what was next. She turned around and got back on top of me reverse cowgirl style. I watched in amazement as her ass moved up and down, while her pussy swallowed my dick over and over again. All I could think about was how good paradise felt and closed my eyes again. Nicole slightly turned her head around, watching me, as she rode me even faster by now. She wanted to see me being pleased which turned her on even more. I knew she would be coming soon.

"Hell yeah, baby, you got momma's pussy feeling real good now!"

"So come on my dick the way you used to."

After yelling out at the top of her lungs, Nicole finally climaxed. She was satisfied and got what she really wanted or at least that's what I thought. After catching her breath, she maneuvered off of my rock-hard dick and began to suck it tasting her cum. Then, facing me, she positioned herself back on top of me.

"Now, Damien, since I got that out the way let me really get to what I wanted to show you."

"What is it now, Nicole? I still want to fuck you some more."

Nicole reached back under the same pillow and pulled out a French chef's knife. The stainless steel blade had to be at least ten inches long as she flashed it in front of me. Then she wrapped both hands around the knife's black handle and reared it over her head.

"I'll show you mother fucker not to toy with my emotions ever again," she said in a sinister way.

"You crazy ass psychotic bitch!" I screamed while unsuccessfully pulling on the handcuffs. "I knew I should have never agreed to meet you here."

"Goodbye Damien Hardy and good riddance to your tired ass!" Nicole shouted out as she thrust the blade towards my chest.

"No!" I cried out as loud as I could.

Everything went pitch black, silent, and I found myself grasping for air. Surprisingly, I opened my eyes to bright sunlight within a room and a familiar voice next to me.

"Damien, are you alright?" asked Diamond as she bent down on the couch I was laying on.

"Huh!" I squalled frantically sitting up and jerking away from her.

"Baby, it's me, Diamond. You were just having a bad dream."

"Oh my God, thank goodness!"

"What in the world were you dreaming about?"

"I think someone was trying to kill me."

"Who was it?"

"I really don't know, Diamond," I said trying to disguise my lie.

"Well, it's all over now," Diamond said standing straight up. "It was just a bad dream you were having while taking a nap."

"Yeah, I realize that now."

"I'm off to pick up Christian from school."

"Okay, I'll see you two later."

"You better get a move on it yourself, Damien. You don't want to be late meeting with your potential client this afternoon."

"Don't worry I won't be late."

"Good luck and I'll see you later this evening," Diamond said kneeling down giving me a kiss. "I love you."

"I love you too, Diamond." I said after we kissed.

I sat there on the couch still startled like the dream was reality. Then I waited for Diamond to travel downstairs and exit the townhome. Momentarily, I found my way to the half-bathroom down the hall. There, I splashed some cold water on my face and patted it dry with a towel. As I looked into the mirror, I straighten up my tie and assured myself I'd never reconnect with Nicole again. She was a distant memory and definitely out of my life. Then, I grabbed my leather portfolio, the keys to my car, and headed out the door.

CHAPTER 2

Diamond pulled her BMW X5 up along the curbside at Christian's school. This was the designated area where parents could pick up their children after school had ended for the day. She exited the vehicle and stood on the side walk as a mass of kids rushed out of the school to their waiting parents. Finally, she noticed a familiar face quickly approaching her.

"There's my handsome son," she said.

"Hi mom," Christian said smiling.

"How was your day?" Diamond asked stooping down to hug her son.

"I had fun today," he replied as he hugged his mother then ended the embrace.

"Aren't you forgetting something, young man?"

"Come on, mom."

"Christian, I'm serious. You owe me a kiss as always."

"Can I wait until we get into the car?"

"Okay, but as soon as we get inside you owe me."

"That's a deal."

Diamond removed herself from her son's side and the pair hopped into the vehicle with tinted windows. Christian now had no hesitations to please his mother.

"Alright, Christian, lay it on me," Diamond said as she leaned her cheek over to her son.

"There are you happy now, mom?" Christian asked as he kissed her lightly on the cheek.

"Yes, I'm always happy when my son gives me a kiss."

"Well, I'm glad I made you happy."

"Why is it so hard for you to give your mother a kiss?"

"I guess being in the fourth grade and watching my friends see me kiss you is kind of embarrassing."

"Oh, Christian, there will be a day in your life when that won't even matter anymore."

"There will?"

Diamond looked at her son as if maybe he was just

too young to understand. Thus, she didn't even attempt to answer his question but rather simply shook her head. The two buckled up and prepared for the journey home. The school's traffic was slow moving as Diamond pulled away from the curb.

"What do you want to eat for dinner tonight, Christian?"

"I really don't know right now."

"I thought you would say pizza or burgers."

"We learned in health class that more kids should eat a well-balanced meal instead of greasy or fatty foods."

"That's good to know your becoming health conscious about what you eat, Christian."

"Plus, eating healthy will make me big and strong. That's what I need in order to make it to the big leagues in baseball."

"Well, speaking about baseball, how about playing in a summer league in Atlanta this year?"

"Aw, mom, do I really have to?"

"Christian, I really think it will be a good experience since school is out in a few weeks."

"Why?"

"For starters, you could have your dad around to act as a hands-on baseball mentor."

"But I was really looking forward to playing in the summer baseball league back in Chicago with all my friends."

"Yes, I understand and your grandparents would love to have you over for the summer again."

"Can I please go back to Chicago for the summer, mom?"

"Okay, Christian, you win. I'll give your grandparents a call and set up everything."

"Alright!"

Diamond wanted the best for her son but didn't want to force anything upon him. She wanted Christian and I to bond even more as any mother would. Ultimately, only time would dictate how close we would eventually become.

The slow moving traffic began to pick up. By now, Christian had pulled out a magazine from his book bag and was glancing through it.

"What are you reading over there?" Diamond asked her son.

"It's just the current issue of *Sports Illustrated*," Christian answered back. "I'm trying to keep up with the latest baseball news since the season just started."

"You really love the sport of baseball and always have," Diamond announced smiling.

"Mom, maybe one day you'll see me on this cover," he said proudly holding up the magazine.

"Let's keep our fingers crossed, Christian, and maybe it will happen."

"Okay mom."

"Hey, I just thought about what we could have for dinner tonight."

"Oh yeah."

"How about if I cook us a taco salad with a few enchiladas?"

"Hmmm, that sounds tasty, mom."

"And it's low in calories and easy to prepare."

"Do you have everything at home to make the meal?"

"Unfortunately not, Christian, but we can make a quick stop at the grocery store."

"That's fine, mom. I'll go inside with you and help pick out all the ingredients to make the meal."

Diamond smiled again as she made a detour before heading home. She knew Christian showed an interest in cooking and most often helped her in the kitchen.

Within a few minutes, the pair had arrived at the grocery store near their home. Christian quickly tucked the *Sports Illustrated* magazine back inside his book bag. Then, they both made their way inside. About fifteen minutes later, mother and son reemerged with Christian carrying a couple of plastic bags filled with food. Both of them entered the vehicle and headed home. Halfway there, Diamond's cell phone began to ring.

"Now, I wonder who that could be?" she asked reaching for her purse which was next to her. Once she had possession of the phone she quickly answered. "Hello."

"Is he there with you?" asked the caller softly on the other end.

"Listen, this is not the right time," replied Diamond attempting to be discreet.

"Well, when the hell is it?" asked the caller in a loud manner.

"I'll have to call you back later," stated Diamond.

Christian had noticed something strange was going on. He glanced away from his magazine to address his mother.

"Mom, is everything okay?"

"Yes, Christian, everything is alright."

Since Christian was assured all was well, he went back to reading his magazine. Diamond continued driving with the cell phone to her ear.

"I'm so tired of you brushing me off every time I

call," announced the caller in a rude tone. "We need to finally get this out in the open for once and for all."

"Like I told you earlier, this is not the right time," Diamond told the caller still attempting to remain calm.

"I'm so damn sick and tired of you trying to sweep this issue under the rug," the caller said sounding agitated.

Diamond had heard enough of what the caller was trying to say. She simply ended the conversation by hanging up the call and turning her cell phone completely off. Then she stuffed it back inside her purse while peeking at Christian. He continued to read his magazine as if he didn't hear a word.

Within a few minutes they made it back home. Diamond pulled the vehicle into the garage of her townhome while Christian stuffed his magazine back into his book bag.

"I'll see you upstairs, mom," Christian said as he opened his door and grabbed the bags full of groceries. "I want to see if there is a baseball game on TV."

"Okay, Christian, I'm right behind you," she said before he darted upstairs out of sight.

Diamond shut off the vehicle's engine as the garage door closed completely down behind her. She picked up her purse, exited the vehicle, and began to walk upstairs.

Suddenly, she paused for a minute and thought about what the caller had said. It was so true, eventually she was going to have to face the music.

CHAPTER 3

It was few minutes before four o'clock as I made my way into Starbucks for my appointment. I arrived early for my meeting and looked around for my potential business client. The quaint sitting area was full of people but I noticed a tall older gentleman standing in the back of the order line. He was wearing a navy blue suit and wore black-colored rimmed glasses. This person fit the exact description of whom I was meeting. Therefore, I promptly made my way up to him.

"Excuse me, sir, are you Mr. White?" I asked the well-dressed man.

"Yes, I am," he exclaimed turning slightly towards me. "And you must be Damien Hardy?"

"Yes sir," I answered offering him a handshake.

"Well, it's finally good to put a face to a name," he said while shaking my hand firmly. "Damien, since we've been formally introduced, please just call me Jamison."

"Will do, Jamison," I said in a pleasant tone.

"I figured we can discuss our business out on the terrace if you don't mind."

"That's perfectly fine. The weather is nice and bearably warm for this time of the year."

"Damien, before we go outside, I wanted to order something to drink."

"That's no problem at all, Jamison. I'll wait in line with you."

"Do you care for something to quench your thirst?"

"I've never really acquired the taste for coffee. Maybe I'll order an orange juice or something."

"Very well, Damien."

As it turned out, Jamison was referred to me by one of my shoe clients from back in the day. She was dejected that I wouldn't be supplying her with any more of the latest high-end designer heels. Fortunate for me, she was ecstatic about helping me to establish my marketing consulting business.

Jamison, who recently moved to Atlanta from

Houston, was a former executive chef turned entrepreneur. After working nearly twenty years in the food industry, most notably with Marriott, he decided to start his own catering business. He wanted me to help develop a marketing strategy to boost sales while generating revenue.

"Can I take your order, sir?" asked the young man behind the register as we finally made it to the front of the counter.

"Ummm let me see," replied Jamison as he looked at the beverage selection in front of him. "I'm debating between the caffe latte and white chocolate mocha."

"They're both excellent choices, sir," said the young man with interest. "But for me, the white chocolate mocha is a personal favorite of mine."

"Okay, then I'll go with the white chocolate mocha," Jamison said taking the young man's suggestion.

"Will that complete your order, sir?"

"Actually add an orange juice to my order as well."

"Yes sir. Give me a second and I'll be right back with your beverages."

The young man turned away to retrieve the order. By now, Jamison pulled his wallet out from his pocket. I thought this would be a perfect time to intervene.

"Here, Jamison, let me pay for the order," I

suggested.

"Oh, you don't have to go through all that, Damien," he announced kindly. "I'll pay for it."

"Are you sure?"

"Absolutely."

The young man finally reappeared with our beverages. Jamison paid for the order as he insisted on and we both made our way out to the terrace. Then it was time to get down to some business.

"So how are you getting accustomed to Atlanta?" I asked trying to initiate some small talk.

"Actually pretty good," he answered as he took a sip from his beverage. "The major hiccup is getting use to all the traffic."

"Yeah, the traffic can be challenging but I think you're going to fall in love with Atlanta."

"Let's hope so."

"Either way, Atlanta is a great opportunity for your catering business," I said opening up my leather portfolio. "You'll see from the reports I generated, you can have a successful and thriving business here."

"I'm anxious to see what you have," he responded.

For the next forty-five minutes or so I extensively explained how my marketing consulting services could benefit Jamison's catering business. He listened extensively as I had documented graphs, charts, and tables outlining my presentation. Overall, I felt the presentation was well received.

"Well, Jamison, that's the essence of how my services can benefit your catering business," I said closing my leather portfolio. "What do you think?"

"I'm quite impressed, Damien," he said.

"I'd love to begin right away helping you. Should I go ahead and draft up the contract?"

"Yes you may, but there is one other issue I'd like to address."

"Sure, I'm listening."

"I have an investor, who acts as a silent partner, in my new company. I would request that you meet him first."

"That's no problem, Jamison. I can even present the same information to him if needed."

"That may not be necessary although he probably will ask you a few questions."

"Is there any anticipated timeframe when we all can meet?"

"Let me consult with him first, but I would assume it should be real soon."

"I'm definitely looking forward to the meeting and

establishing a sound business relationship with you."

"And I look forward to utilizing your professional services, Damien."

We ended our meeting with a customary firm handshake. I happily walked Jamison outside where we exchanged a few more words. Then he departed and so did I.

The evening traffic was in full swing by the time I left Starbucks. I was closer to my condo on Lenox Road so I decided to retire there for the evening instead of going back to Diamond's place. While sitting in traffic, I thought it would be a good time to call Diamond. I quickly picked up my cell phone and dialed her number. Shortly, she answered my call.

"Hello."

"Hey, Diamond, it's me."

"Hi, baby," she said with enthusiasm. "How did the meeting go with Mr. White?"

"It was awesome," I replied while maneuvering though the thick traffic. "He was very pleased and wants me to meet with his investor."

"That's great, Damien, I'm really proud of you."

"Well, the deals not closed yet, but hopefully it will be soon."

"Don't worry I know it will happen for you."

"Well, what are you up to now?"

"I'm in the kitchen cooking enchiladas and taco salad for dinner."

"That sounds tasty."

"Aren't you coming over here to eat dinner with us?"

"It's been a long day and plus I'm stuck in traffic right now. I think I'm going to just head back to my place."

"I made plenty for you also, Damien. Are you sure?"

"Yeah, I'm positive, Diamond. I'll grab something quick to eat before I get home."

"Okay, if you insist, but there is one other thing I wanted to discuss with you."

"Sure, what is it?"

"Christian told me he would rather go back to Chicago for the summer. He wants to play in the baseball summer league there."

"Maybe that's the best thing for him especially if he wants to do that."

"You're not disappointed?"

"There's no reason to be disappointed, Diamond. There will be plenty of summers in the future."

"Well, I'm glad you're fine with him going to Chicago for the summer."

"Where is Christian anyway?"

"He's in the living room watching television. Hold on for a second and I'll let you talk to him."

Diamond left the kitchen, with phone in hand, and walked to the living room. There, Christian was immersed into a baseball game on the TV. His mother handed him the phone letting him know it was me.

"Hi, dad," Christian said grabbing the phone.

"Hey, All-Star," I responded back. "What are you doing?"

"I'm watching the Cubs game on TV."

"Who are they playing?"

"They're playing the Pirates, and up by two runs in the six inning."

"It seems like they're on their way to another victory."

"I sure hope so, dad. Hey, did my mom tell you about me going back to Chicago for the summer?"

"Yeah, I'm really excited about you playing in the summer league up there again."

"Me too. I can't wait to see all my friends again."

"But promise me one thing, Christian."

"What's that, dad?"

"That you'll earn the MVP award like you did last summer."

"You got it, dad, I promise."

"Well, kiss your mom for me and I'll talk with you two later."

"Okay, I'll see you later, dad."

The call between us ended and I did a great job not letting him know I was disappointed. I really wanted him to play baseball here in Atlanta this summer but I guess we all make sacrifices. Even more disappointing was the traffic I was currently stuck in. I removed my tie and took a deep breath. It was evident I wasn't going anywhere for a while.

CHAPTER 4

"Oh, lawd, don't you dare talk about my bishop up in here!" Raphael shouted emphatically as he paused styling Wanda's hair. "I still love him no matter what."

"Raphael, don't get mad at me," said Wanda. She continued to look at her fabulous hair from the mirror in front of her. She remained calm and seated in her chair as Raphael looked at her in an awkward way.

Diamond stilled owned Styles Salon on Piedmont Road and this Saturday was no different from any other. The place was packed with women getting their weaves tighten up for the weekend. Raphael was still the best stylist in the entire elegant establishment. On this particular day, he had one of his regular customers sitting in his chair as he worked on her hair. Within the waiting area, plenty of women eagerly waited for their turn.

Today, he was dressed in a pair of designer skinny-legged jeans with heels on of course. He wore a sexy contour-fitting shirt which showed off his six-four two-hundred and twenty pound athletic and muscular frame. To bolster his attire, he added a polka dot pink scarf around his neck.

"Chi, don't you start that mess today,"

"Well, I ain't starting it, I'm just reporting what's being said."

"We all come short of his glory and Bishop Eddie Wrong is not exempt," said Raphael as he gathered his composure. Then he rolled his eyes and continued working on Wanda's hair.

"The way he denounced homosexuality every Sunday to his congregation you thought he'd be exempt," announced Wanda. "Now, look at him. He turned out to be just another down low brother."

"Girl stop, you know I already knew that. I can spot them a mile away."

"Yeah, Raphael, I figured you would know."

Around this time, the streets of Atlanta were buzzing about Bishop Eddie Wrong and his mega church congregation in Lithonia. For years, he was labeled as the most homophobic preacher in America. He adamantly rejected homosexuality and didn't mind openly discussing it whenever he could. Now, there was a scandal brewing how he manipulated the word and church by having sexual interaction with younger boys in his congregation. Being that he was married for over thirty years and had four children didn't fair too well in the black community. Pending criminal and civil litigation didn't stop lewd photos of him and these young boys from surfacing on the internet. So you can only image that Bishop Eddie Wrong was the hottest topic in every beauty and barber shop in Atlanta.

"Now, Wanda let me know what you think," said Raphael stepping away from his client.

"Lawd have mercy, Raphael, you did the damn thang!" she exclaimed looking at her new hairdo in the mirror. "Hands down you are the best stylist in the ATL."

"Chi please, tell me something I don't know."

"Let me give you your money so I can get out of here. I'm going be looking good for my man tonight."

"Girl, don't you dare let him sweat that perfect hair style out tonight," Raphael said as he began to remove the cape from around Wanda. "Otherwise, you'll be right back in here on Monday."

"Oh, hell no," Wanda responded. "He knows better than to touch my hair especially after I had it done. He can only get it from the back or he won't get it at all."

"That's what I'm talking about, girl," remarked Raphael as Wanda stood up from the chair. "Head down ass up is always the best way."

"Raphael, stop that!" Wanda silently shouted as she gave him a playful pat on his shoulder.

The two embraced in a hug with a smile. Then Raphael prepared his work station for his next client. Meanwhile, Wanda dug into her purse and paid Raphael which included a generous tip. Within two weeks, she would be back in the salon like clockwork.

Tameka, who was the salon's receptionist, directed Raphael's next client to move over to his work station. The eager and now happy woman rose up from her seat in the plush waiting area. Before she could get halfway to Raphael, in bolts Katrina through the front door and almost knocked Wanda over as she walked out. She quickly rushed over to Raphael.

"Raphael, I desperately need to see you right away," pleaded Katrina.

"Ma'am," shouted Tameka rising from her chair at the reception desk. "We are an appointment only salon.

Besides, there are a few people in front of you."

"I'm actually next," said the woman, who was scheduled with Raphael, as she took a seat in his chair. "Plus I've been waiting for nearly two hours already."

"We'll see about that," proclaimed Katrina as she marched up to Tameka's desk.

"Ma'am, I'm sorry but Raphael is already booked for the rest of the day," explained Tameka. "I can see if another stylist can fit you in."

"No, that won't suffice," Katrina said with conviction. Then she reached in her purse and slammed her black card on Tameka's desk. "Whatever I want I get. I'll pay for the woman's hair style sitting in Raphael's chair plus the women waiting behind her. And I'll add in a thirty percent gratuity but I need Raphael to see me now."

"Oh, she wants to pay for my hair style," said the woman getting out of Raphael's chair. Then she walked over to Tameka's desk. "I don't have any squabbles about that."

The other women in the waiting area didn't mind either. And just like that Katrina got her way as usual.

"You can tally up the bill and bring my card back to me," ordered Katrina. Then she made her way to Raphael's work station and took a seat.

Katrina Hope was a middle-aged power woman who was classy, attractive, brash, and anal all rolled into one. This was probably why she didn't have a man since she always thought she was running the show. She was a partner at the prestigious law firm McLaughlin, Hope, Berkowitz, and Lee located in downtown Atlanta. Her firm handled high profile celebrity criminal cases and corporate civil claims. Katrina's motto was 'if it doesn't make dollars then it doesn't make sense' and she meant it with a passion. As usual, she always walked with swag and kept her head in the clouds as if her shit didn't stink.

"Oh, honey, where have you been?" asked Raphael as he placed a cape around Katrina.

"In civil litigation hell if you can imagine that," Katrina answered. "I have an emergency motion to argue in front of my constituents but most importantly with Judge Tanner. I need to look picture perfect and flawless as usual on Monday morning."

"Well you definitely came to the right place because you know I'm going to make you look like a doll."

"Yes, I do know that, Raphael."

"So, who did this here?" Raphael asked running his fingers though Katrina's hair.

"Raphael, I was in Chicago for legal business

recently and my girlfriend recommended a stylist for me," Katrina answered. "Apparently, the stylist did an okay job."

"More like a hot ass mess in my opinion."

"I'm constantly in and out of major cities and it so hard to find a great stylist."

"Yeah, I know what you mean. Everyone claiming to be the best ain't always the best."

"Maybe you should come with me on a few of my business trips, Raphael. Then, I wouldn't run into this problem."

"What cities do you normally travel to?"

"It's mostly Chicago, New York, and occasionally Los Angeles."

"Well, I'd love to travel with you back to my hometown of Los Angeles," exclaimed Raphael.

"I'll definitely make it happen," Katrina said. "It would be such a perk to have my own personal stylist to make me glamorous for my big legal cases."

"Now, honey, you know I'm not cheap."

"Raphael, you know I'm not either."

"Darling, I'm so excited," Raphael said with excitement. "I get to travel with a diva and get paid."

"Yes, Raphael," said Katrina smiling. "You're well worth it."

After their brief conversation, Raphael suggested a few styles to Katrina that would be perfect for her legal argument. He suggested something bold and sexy but still conservative. He wanted her hair to be exquisite in the courtroom while she looked classy and sophisticated. Katrina took every suggestion into consideration. Then she made a tough decision on which style she wanted.

After nearly two grueling hours, Raphael had washed, cut, and styled Katrina's hair to where it was pictured perfect. He even added a few extensions to give her hair more body and fullness. It was obvious she was pleased because she couldn't stop smiling in the mirror in front of her.

By now, Tameka had walked over to Raphael's work station and politely handed Katrina her card back. Katrina didn't even turn towards her but simply held her hand out while looking forward in the mirror.

"Here you are, ma'am," Tameka said depositing the plastic in Katrina's hand. "As you requested, I charged your card for your service plus the additional women as well."

"Um hum," Katrina muttered as if it was no big deal. Then she stuffed the card back into her purse.

"Enjoy the rest of your day, ma'am," Tameka said

as she turned around and rolled her eyes.

"Damn, Raphael, you are one piece of work!" Katrina said standing up from the chair. "I just love my new hair style."

"Yes, darling, and you wear it so well," Raphael said as he removed the cape from her. Then her grabbed a lint brush and began to rub it over the shoulders of her outfit. "Now, you look like you're going to knock 'em dead on Monday morning."

"You can definitely say that again," responded Katrina as she reached down into her purse. She pulled out a fifty dollar bill and handed it to Raphael. "Here's a little something extra for all your efforts."

"Oh, thank you, boo!" Raphael exclaimed and then gave her a hug.

The other women, in the waiting area, noticed how flawless Katrina looked. But deep down inside they already knew they would never look like her.

"One other thing before I go, Raphael."

"Yes, darling."

"How's your cousin Damien doing lately?"

"He's great, Katrina. He finally got his marketing consulting business off the ground."

"Well, that's great to hear even though I miss my

designer shoes."

"I'll let him know you asked about him."

"Yeah, you do that. I'll see you next time."

"Chow."

Katrina turned towards the front entrance and strutted forward. Before reaching the door, she slightly glanced over at the women in the waiting area and turned her nose up at them. Once outside, she jumped into her grey convertible Bentley Continental GT. As always, she took off like a rocket as if her shit didn't stink.

CHAPTER 5

"How much further till we get there, mom?" yelled Christian from the back seat.

"We're almost there, Christian," replied Diamond as she slightly turned her head around from the front passenger seat.

"Don't worry, All-Star, I'll get you to the airport on time," I added as I maneuvered Diamond's BMW X5 through the downtown connector.

"I can't wait to get back to Chicago," Christian said with emphasis. He had his favorite baseball glove on his left hand while punching the middle part of the glove with his opposite hand. "I'm anxious to see all my friends and get stated with the baseball summer league."

School has officially ended and as we all agreed

Christian was to spend the summer in Chicago. While in Chicago, he would stay with Diamond's parents. He was now eleven years old and I convinced Diamond he would be okay flying by himself for the two hour trip. Christian was super-excited and thought it was real cool that he would be on an airplane without his mother. I reassured Diamond the airline would have a personal flight attendant to make sure Christian would be alright. But during our drive, I could tell Diamond was still nervous.

"Well, we finally made it," I said as I pulled into the Delta Airlines' Terminal.

"Alright!" Christian softly screamed out raising both arms in the air.

"Now, I just need to find a place to park and we can head inside to the concourse," I added.

Luckily, I only had to drive around for a few moments before I finally found a place to park. Like always, Hartsfield-Jackson Airport was crowded as usual. It didn't matter what day of the week it was, the airport was always hustle and bustle. After securing a parking spot, we all exited the vehicle.

"We did great on time," Diamond said as she looked at her watch. "We still have a little over two hours before Christian's flight leaves."

"I'll just grab his luggage from the back," I exclaimed. "Then we can all head inside."

After retrieving Christian's single suitcase, I locked the vehicle and we all moved forward. Christian walked next to his mother with his book bag on his shoulders and glove in hand. I followed closely behind the pair carrying the light suitcase.

From the rear, Diamond was looking stunning as always. She was dressed fashionably casual but was working it. On her feet were her favorite four-inch Gucci heels. She wore designer skinny-legged jeans that hugged her nice ass. And as always, her protruding breasts drew attention to the saffron material shirt. The wind blew through her shoulder-length dark blonde hair as I thought how lucky I was to have her. Even a few gentlemen noticed her beauty and smiled.

Normally, only ticket holders are allowed in the gate area where the flights depart. Since Christian was flying solo, the airport made an exception and allowed us to travel with him to this area. Once we were in the gate area, we all took a seat in the waiting section where other passengers were. By now, there was still about an hour and a half until his flight departed.

"I'm going to hate to see my baby leave without

me," said Diamond as she put her arm around her son.

"Don't worry, mom," Christian announced. "I'm going to be okay."

"I know, baby, but every mother always worries about their child."

"Well, I'm going to make you proud of me this summer."

"I'm already proud of you, Christian."

"I know, mom, but I'm going to make you more proud of me."

"Oh really."

"Yeah, that's right."

"How?"

"I'm going to win the MVP in the baseball summer league again just like last year."

"Okay, I'm going to hold you to that. But either way, I still love you the same."

"I love you too, mom."

After an extended period, there was an announcement we all had been waiting to hear. Over the intercom, in the waiting area, a soft voice began to speak.

"Ladies and gentlemen, may I please have your attention," announced the pleasant voice. "We will now begin boarding flight 3301 to Chicago at gate C. Please remember to have your identification and boarding pass present when you reach the gate."

"Well, All-Star, that's our cue," I said rising from my seat. "Let's make our way over to gate C."

Christian hopped up out of his seat eagerly and Diamond followed. Then the three of us made our way over to the boarding area where a line began to form. We all patiently waited in line until a young and attractive flight attendant made her way towards us.

"You must be Christian," said the flight attendant smiling.

"Yes, ma'am, I am," he replied.

"Hello, I'm Jenni your personal chaperone for the flight today," she said extending her hand to his.

"Glad to meet you, Jenni," Christian said shaking her hand.

"Hello, ma'am," Jenni said to Diamond. Then she calmly shook her hand as well.

"Hi, Jenni," Diamond replied. "I'm Christian's mother."

"And I'm Damien," I interjected quickly as the two ended their hand embrace. Jenni and I shook hands as well.

"Now, don't you two worry," Jenni said. "We're going to treat Christian with V.I.P. status until he arrives in

Chicago.

"What's V.I.P.?" asked Christian.

"That means you're a very important person today, Christian," Diamond answered.

"That's right," Jenni continued. "And for starters that means you don't have to wait in this long line. Now, let's make our way to the front of the line. There we can get you on the plane."

All three of us followed Jenni near the front of the line. That's when Diamond submitted Christian's identification and boarding pass for verification. During this time, I knelt down on one knee to say farewell to Christian.

"Now, make sure you listen to your grandparents during your stay in Chicago," I said firmly looking into his eyes. "Make us proud by bringing back that MVP trophy."

"You betcha, dad," Christian said with a big smile on his face.

I hugged my son to let him know I was proud of him. Whether or not he brought back the MVP trophy, I would still love him the same. Before I stood up, I realized I needed to give him something. I reached within the inside pocket of my jacket.

"I forgot to give this to you earlier," I said handing

him his hair brush. "You're definitely going to need this because appearance is everything."

"Hey, where did you get my brush?" Christian asked taking possession of it.

"You left it on the bathroom counter at your mother's house," I answered. "I found it right before we left."

"Oh okay," he said and then stuffed it into his book bag.

After our exchange of words, I stood up. Jenni had just finished everything up with Diamond.

"Okay, Christian, give me a hug and a kiss," ordered Diamond turning to her son.

"Mom, not again," Christian complained.

"No, I don't want to hear that tired excuse again."

"Alright you win, mom."

With only a little bit of hesitation, Christian showed great emotion as he hugged and kissed his mother. Diamond hugged him extra hard and had to fight shedding a few tears. Then she regained her composure and turned back towards Jenni.

"Make sure you take good care of my baby," Diamond exclaimed as she faced Jenni.

"Don't worry, ma'am," Jenni responded. "He will

be in good hands with us.

Christian was eager to grab the young and pretty flight attendant's hand. Together, they walked down the corridor leading to the plane. As the pair got further away, Christian suddenly turned around and waved. Diamond and I waved back as we stood side by side in an embrace. Shortly, he was out of our sight and that was the last time we would see him for a while.

CHAPTER 6

"C'mon, baby, cheer up," I said as we traveled back through the downtown connector headed to Sandy Springs. "It's not that bad."

"I know, Damien," Diamond said sadly while she looked out her window. "It's not our first time apart but when we are I miss him so much."

"That just proves you're a great mother to Christian but eventually he's going to be a grown man."

"Yeah, that's the day I'm dreading the most."

"How about I cook you something nice to eat when we get back to your place," I said glancing over to her.

"You mean you can cook?" Diamond asked finally turning away from the window while giving me a serious look.

"Yes, I can burn a little something now and then."

"I never pictured you as a chef, Damien."

"Well, I had to learn to cook a little, Diamond. Eating out every day as a bachelor can get expensive."

"Okay, I'm anxious to see this."

"I bet you are."

"What are you going to cook for me, Damien?"

"It's a surprise, baby."

"That's fine because I just love surprises."

After whizzing through the light Atlanta traffic, we finally arrived back safely at Diamond's townhome. Once we were inside the gated community, I quickly maneuvered the vehicle into Diamond's garage. Then we both exited the SUV and made our way up to the second floor. There, I headed straight for the kitchen and put on an apron as if I really was a world-class chef. Diamond moved to the living room and began playing some soft R&B music on the stereo system. The tunes were mellow and relaxing.

I opened the door to the stainless-steel refrigerator to see what I could conjure up for us. The last thing I wanted to do was put my foot in my mouth and disappoint Diamond. The first thing I noticed was an unopened bottle of Moscato so I grabbed it. I figured Diamond could use a drink to calm her nerves and take the worries off her mind.

Quickly, I found a cork screw and two glasses. Before I had a chance to call Diamond into the kitchen, she suddenly appeared.

"Damien, I'm going to take a calm and relaxing bath while you cook us something to eat."

"That's fine, baby, but I want you to take this glass of wine with you."

"You must have read my mind."

"Yeah, I'm pretty good at that."

Diamond took the glass from my hand and placed it to her luscious lips. Slowly, she took a sip and then another.

"Now, are you sure you don't need my help in here, Damien?"

"Yes, baby, I'll be fine. Just go ahead and take your soothing bath."

"Okay, I'll be back in about half an hour and pray the kitchen won't be on fire."

"Don't worry it won't be."

"Well, give me a kiss before I leave, Damien."

"Anything for you, baby."

I inched closer to Diamond and gave her a nice soft kiss. Then I repeated the process again. Soon I found my arms wrapped around her waist. My hands slowly descending to her thick and fine ass. I grabbed and squeezed it while moving her even closer to me.

"Wait, Damien, we'll have plenty of time for that," Diamond said moving a little bit away from me. "Besides, you're supposed to be cooking now."

"Yeah, you're right," I said trying to not sound disappointed. "Go ahead and take your bath and I'll see you shortly."

Before Diamond left, she gave me a quick peck on the lips. Then she disappeared to the third floor of the townhome where the master bedroom and bath suite was located.

By now, it was do or die because I had to figure out what to cook. I thought about my grandmother, who raised me, back in Los Angeles. She was as great woman but one helluva cook. I asked myself what would she cook in a situation like this and one dish came to mind. It was cream Cajun chicken pasta consisting of N'awlin style Alfredo sauce. Since we were of Caribbean descent, Cajun food was her specialty and she went out of her way to teach me how to cook a dish or two. This particular meal was quick, simple, and most importantly romantic.

Luckily for me, Diamond had all the items and ingredients within her refrigerator. While the soft music continued to play, I boiled the linguine then seasoned two boneless and skinless chicken breasts. After that, I chopped up green onions, tomatoes, and even grated some parmesan cheese. Once everything was prepped, I carefully prepared the meal. The final step included the food simmering on the stove for about thirty-five minutes. During this time, I stepped back and grabbed my glass of wine and took a sip.

"My, my, my you definitely have it really smelling good in here," Diamond said standing in the entrance to the kitchen.

She caught me off guard as I looked around. What was even more surprising was the outfit she was wearing. There she stood caramel complexion looking sexy in her four-inch Gucci heels wearing nothing but laced lingerie panties and bra.

"Damn, baby, you sure look tasty right about now," I said as I took another sip from my glass.

"Well, you're more than welcomed to taste this appetizer before the main meal."

"I think I'll do just that."

Diamond grabbed my hand and led the way to the living room. On the way there, I had my eyes fixed on her perfectly shaped and sexy derriere. It swayed from side to side as she walked.

Once we reached our destination, Diamond made

me sit in the middle of the plush leather sofa. I placed my glass of wine on the end table next to me. Then she stepped on the large cocktail table and began to perform for me. She danced eloquently with the soft music and slowly turned all around for me. Not missing a beat with the music, I was enthralled that she was my private and personal dancer. Finally, she faced me again and extended her hands to her head. Then she gyrated her hips in a circular motion inviting me to come and get it.

Before I could stand up, she slowly turned around not missing a beat with the music. She taunted me with her backside towards me. Then all of a sudden, she spread her legs apart and kept them straight. Slowly she bent down and touched her toes while her ass jiggled. I couldn't take it anymore.

With my hard dick and all, I stood up and moved closer to her. Diamond remained in the same position while I unstrapped her bra as it quickly fell onto the floor. Then I delicately moved her panties all the way down to her ankles. Without a struggle to balance, she lifted her left heel off the table so I could continue to remove her panties. Then she repeated the process with her right heel. Afterwards, I grabbed her ankles and slowly moved my hands upwards. When they reached her backside, I slightly bent down, spread her ass, and commenced to lick her clit. She continued to shake her ass and moved letting me know she loved what I was doing. With my tongue, I licked her pussy walls and then stopped near her anus. After I thought she had enough, I got back on her clit again.

Diamond was almost there but I wasn't going to let her come just yet. I made her stand straight up, and then carried her in my arms over to the sofa. As if she was fragile, I lay her there and kneeled down. She already knew what to do by quickly spreading open her legs. I latched on to her clit this time and didn't let go. I repeatedly sucked it over and over again. While this was going on, I inserted my index and middle fingers into her pussy. I then moved my fingers in a back and forth motion. As her pussy got wetter, I inserted my ring finger. There I was sucking the hell out of her clit and forcing my fingers into her wet pussy faster and faster. Diamond loved it and began to scream and moan.

"Oh, that's right, Damien, suck your pussy real good," she yelled out with her head arched back and eyes closed.

"You like the way I'm eating my pussy?" I asked as I came up for air.

"Hell yeah, baby."

"Well, then be quiet and let me continue."

I went back down but this time with more passion. I licked and sucked while penetrating faster. Within a few seconds, her cum was oozing all on my fingers. Once it all had excreted from her, I withdrew my fingers. I placed my tongue where my fingers once were and made sure to lick up any remaining cum. Then I place all three fingers inside Diamond's mouth.

"Doesn't your cum taste good, baby?" I asked as I stopped licking her pussy momentarily.

"Yes, Damien, it does," she repeated making sure to lick all my fingers.

Diamond's legs began to quiver and shake as her explosion was physically draining. I took both hands and held both legs up and apart so I could finish licking any remaining cum in between her. Then I stood straight up and reached for my glass of Moscato. After taking a sip, I lowered the glass to my rock hard eight-inched length dick. Carefully, I placed my dick inside the glass and submerged my dick's head into the wine. Then I motioned for Diamond to sit up on the sofa. She gladly placed my dick into her mouth and sucked it with passion.

"Doesn't my dick taste so much better with Moscato on it?" I asked sarcastically.

"Yes, baby, it does," she replied after briefly removing it from her mouth.

I repeated the process of dipping my dick into the glass of Moscato a few more times and letting Diamond taste it. I could tell she was enjoying sucking my dick especially with the great-tasting wine on it. After that task was completed, I put the glass back on the end table. Then, I sat back on the sofa with my hard dick pointing straight up.

"Now, get your sexy ass on top of my dick," I ordered.

"It's about time you told me so," Diamond said slowly as she moved upwards attempting to take off her Gucci heels.

"Oh no you don't, keep them sexy heels on for me."

"Yes, baby."

As I commanded, Diamond faced me and slid her extremely wet pussy all the way down on my dick. Methodically, she began to ride me as the pain turned into pleasure.

"Faster and harder," I screamed as I slapped her ass.

"Oh, yeah, baby, that's what I like!" she screamed back.

"Make my pussy swallow all your dick, girl," I

announced while I grabbed her ass thrusting it down on my dick.

"I'm making your pussy swallow my dick, baby," she yelled out.

"Faster dammit."

"Oh, you're going to make me put some cum on your dick, Damien."

"That's your dick, baby."

"Yes, Damien, that's all my dick."

"Then, put some cum on your dick, dammit."

Diamond did as I ordered and rode me faster than ever. My dick, or should I say her dick, was easily flowing in and out of her. I knew she was almost there because she was going super fast by now.

"Damien, here's your cum, baby!" she screamed out.

"That's good, baby," I exclaimed in excitement. "I'm right behind you."

"Oh, I feel that hot cum skeeting inside me, Damien."

"I told you it was on the way."

Fully exhausted, Diamond rested her torso on my chest. Then she gave me a kiss for the great work I just put in. I didn't let her rest any longer and demanded she get off my dick. She knelt down by the sofa and sucked all the juices off my dick which was still rock hard. Watching her do that kept me erect even longer. After that task was completed, we both lay on the sofa and cuddled. By now, the simmering food was beginning to scorch on the stove but we didn't care. Shortly later, Diamond parents called stating Christian had arrived safely in Chicago. By now, Diamond's mind was fully at ease.

CHAPTER 7

I paused, for a moment, as I sat in my bimmer thinking about the next move. The engine was still idling for a while when I finally grabbed the key and turned the car completely off. In front of me were a set of single-level office buildings discretely tucked away off Peachtree Road. Once I had enough courage, I grabbed the small bag on the passenger seat and decided now was the time.

After walking a few yards from my vehicle, I entered one of the quaint office buildings. Inside, I noticed a petite sitting area but no one was there. Slightly in front of me was a waist-high counter with a sliding-glass partition.

"May I help you, sir?" asked the woman standing up as she slid the glass back a little.

"Um, yes you can," I answered nervously as I walked forward to her. "I called a few days ago and spoke to someone named Courtney."

"I'm Courtney," she said rather quickly.

"Oh, hi Courtney," I said still sounding nervous. "You probably don't remember speaking with me but I'm Damien."

"Actually, I do remember speaking with you Damien especially with the particular situation you had mentioned."

"Okay, great, then I don't have to explain it to anyone again."

"No, I have you covered."

"Well, I specifically followed the directions you gave me over the phone and brought the items in."

I quickly placed the small bag on the counter. The bag was made of genuine leather which prevented anyone from seeing through it. Inside, there were two additional bags containing some precious items.

"Great, are the items in here?" Courtney asked pointing at the bag on the counter.

"Yes they are," I replied as I began to unzip the bag. "I even carefully separated and labeled the items."

"There is no need to show me," Courtney said

preventing my hand from unzipping the bag. "Now, we just need you to fill out some paperwork."

She reached below the counter from where she was standing and pulled out a clipboard. Attached to it were a few sheets of paper and an ink pen. Then she handed it all to me.

"Wow, I didn't know all this paperwork would be needed."

"Don't worry, Damien, it's not as bad as it looks. Besides, paperwork is standard protocol."

"Okay, I'll grab a seat and get started."

"While you're filling out the paperwork, I'll keep your bag with me behind the counter until you return."

"That's no problem."

"Just come back up to the counter and give me a holler when you're done."

"Sure thing, Courtney."

After our brief exchange of words, I departed from the counter and took a seat. After I sat down, I noticed Courtney had closed the sliding-glass partition and disappeared. To my surprise, I was still the only one in the tiny waiting area but I was glad. Reading through the paperwork, I filled out every section completely and thoroughly as I could. It seemed like too much information to be giving but who was I to question their protocol.

Within fifteen minutes, I finally finished filling out the paperwork. Then I read my answers carefully one more time. Once I determined everything was correct, I walked back up to the counter. There, I quietly knocked on the sliding-glass partition where Courtney suddenly appeared.

"You're all done?" she asked.

"Yes, I am," I answered handing her the clipboard.

"I see you answered every question as best you could."

"Yeah, I tried to be as precise as possible."

"Okay, Damien, the only remaining item is the usual and customary fee."

"I believe you quoted me two-hundred and seventy-five dollars when I called."

"Yes, that is correct."

I retrieved my wallet from my rear pants pocket and gave Courtney my credit card. She scanned the card through their computer system to finalize the transaction. After I signed the credit card receipt, she gave me additional copies of pertinent paperwork.

"Well, there you are Damien, that's all we need for now," Courtney said. "We'll begin the process immediately and should have the results for you soon."

"When should I expect to hear something?" I asked.

"It normally takes a few weeks but I'll give you a call as soon as I have the results."

"Okay, thanks for all your help."

"No problem, Damien, I'll talk with you soon."

I exited the small office building and made my way back to my vehicle. Once I was inside my bimmer, I revved up the engine and peeled out quickly from the parking lot. There was a sigh of relief as I finally got that out of the way. But now I would be anxious to see how everything would turn out.

I arrived back at my condo located on Lenox Road. I bypassed the elevators and jogged up the flight of stairs to the twelfth floor. Fumbling with my keys and breathing heavily, I opened the door to my dwelling.

"Whew," I said out loud to myself as I closed the door behind me. "I remember when I could clear those flight of stairs and not even flinch. I must be getting old."

After walking to the living room, I quickly found the remote and turned the television to the jazz music channel. I needed to hear something relaxing before my daily workout routine. While the music played, I entered my bedroom and quickly changed into my workout attire.

Once I had my throwback Nike Air Max shoes,

fleece jogging pants, and athletic fitted tee shirt on it was time to head out. I grabbed my workout towel and a lemon-lime Gatorade from the refrigerator. I also turned off the television and prepared to head for the gym located on the second floor. Suddenly, my cell phone rang which was still lying on my bed. In a hurry, I retrieved it off the bed and made my way to the front door. Before exiting, I answered the call.

"Hello, this is Damien," I said in my professional tone.

"Hi, Damien, it's me Jamison," said the caller on the other end. "I finally had a chance to follow up with you."

"Oh, hello Jamison," I responded trying not to sound noticeably excited. "I was actually planning on following up with you later this week."

"Well, seems like I beat you to the punch, Damien," he remarked.

"How have things been going for you, Jamison?"

"Pretty good I can't complain."

"That's always good to hear."

"And how have you been, Damien?"

"Actually, everything is well, Jamison. I was headed to the gym for my daily workout routine."

"Man, I wish I could be consistent on working out. I never seem to have enough time in the day."

"It's mind over matter that usually does the trick for me."

"Well, I have to use that the next time I think about evading a good workout. In any event, let me get to the point of why I called you."

"I assume we're one step closer to executing the contract for my services."

"Yes we are Damien but as we discussed my investor is now ready to meet you."

"That's great news, Jamison. So when can we all meet?"

"How about two weeks from this coming Thursday at two o'clock in the afternoon?"

"That works for me, Jamison. I don't have any appointments scheduled that far out."

"Are you familiar with Prime Restaurant in Buckhead?"

"Yes, it's an upscale establishment known quite well for steaks, sushi, and seafood."

"Great, we all can meet there for a late lunch."

"I'll be well prepared to explain my services again."

"My investor is primarily concerned about meeting

the person soliciting the service. Although, you may not have to go in depth about what you can offer like our initial visit."

"Well, don't you worry Jamison. Either way I'll be prepared."

"I'm sure you won't disappoint us, Damien. I'll talk with you soon."

Jamison and I ended our conversation which went very well. I felt great all my hard work of having my own business was beginning to pay off. Now, with good news my workout would be a piece of cake. Quickly, I opened my front door and headed downstairs to the gym.

PART II

SECOND CHANCE

CHAPTER 8

It was late Friday afternoon and I completed a few sales calls to potential clients. Earlier in the day, I even met with someone who was interested in my services. Overall, the day was very productive. Since I had abandoned my former hustle everything was working out fine with my new business.

Now, most people in the ATL are looking forward to happy hour or hitting the hottest clubs around this time. I, on the other hand, never was too fond of drinking or hanging out. So I decided to spend the rest of the evening with my good friend, Mookie. I called him earlier in the day and told him once I finished up I would come over. He was excited and glad we could be able to talk and catch up on some things. Over the last few months, I hadn't spoken to him as much as I would have liked to but I assumed everything was alright.

By the time I made the trek from my condo in Buckhead to his mom's home in Decatur it was shortly after five o'clock. On my way there, I even drove down Candler Road to check out my old neighborhood and stomping grounds. Not much had changed and even the parking lot of South Dekalb Mall was bustling with traffic.

When I arrived at my destination, I parked my car in the spacious driveway, exited my vehicle, and headed up the front porch. As I prepared to ring the doorbell, out comes Mookie's mom, Mrs. Wysinger. She was still the same as ever always looking attractive and dainty.

"Well, look who's here," she said fully exiting the house and closing the door behind her. "Damien, how have you been?"

"I'm great, Mrs. Wysinger," I answered as we both hugged. "And how about yourself?"

"Oh, I'm doing well," she replied as we ended our embrace. "Damien, what brings you over to this side of town?"

"I thought I'd come over and chat with my good friend," I answered and smiled.

"That's so nice of you, Damien. I hope you continue to come over more often."

"Yes, Mrs. Wysinger, that shouldn't be a problem."

"Damien, that's good to hear because my son has been on the straight and narrow since he left that dreaded place. I think you're a positive influence for him."

"Well, that's what real friends are for, Mrs. Wysinger."

"You can go inside, Damien," she exclaimed tucking her medium-sized purse on her shoulder. "I'm headed to the grocery store and will be back shortly."

"Okay," I simply said moving past her and closer to the front door.

"Oh, by the way, what are you doing for dinner tonight?" she suddenly asked pausing before exiting the porch.

"I really don't have any plans," I responded.

"Then stay and have dinner with us tonight."

"Sure, what's on the menu?"

"I'm having fried Cajun flavored catfish, hand-battered onion rings, and my homemade hush puppies."

"Mrs. Wysinger, you already have my mouth watering. That sounds so delicious I wouldn't ever turn that down."

"I think you'll like it, Damien. Besides, it's not too extravagant for a Friday night dinner."

"Well, I've tasted your cooking before and know you can really get down in the kitchen."

We both laughed because she knew I was right even though she tried to remain humble about it. Mrs. Wysinger eventually made her way down the front porch and to her car in the driveway. I remained at the front door making sure she would depart safely. As she entered her vehicle, she spoke again.

"Now, you go ahead and make yourself at home, Damien," she announced. "I'll see you two in a little bit."

"Alright, Mrs. Wysinger," I said waving at her.

Before long, she pulled her car out of the driveway and slowly headed down the street. I closed the front door behind me as I entered the home. Straight ahead of me, past the kitchen, Mookie sat outside on the patio. Eagerly, I made my way to him. When I finally reached him outside, I kind of caught him off guard. He sat there enjoying the simple outdoor life.

"What's up, Mookie!" I shouted.

"Damien, my main man," he said standing up from his chair. "What's happening?"

"Nothing much, bro," I answered as I gave him our

manly handshake and hug. "I'm just maintaining and glad I'm able to do that."

"As long as your free, bro, you can't complain," was his simple suggestion to me.

I pulled up a chair closer to Mookie and we both sat down. I noticed he had a glass of his favorite beverage next to his chair.

"Amen to that, Mookie," I said looking around. "You out here just chillin', huh?"

"Yeah, pretty much so, Damien," he answered and then picked up his glass. "You care for some fresh brewed ice tea?"

"Nah, I'm cool, man. I think I'm going to save as much room in my stomach for the awesome meal your mom is going to make."

"She must have told you what she was planning on cooking?"

"Yeah, right before I came inside she did."

"There's nothing like a good home cooked meal from a woman, Damien."

"Well, speaking about women, how are you and Nadine getting along?"

"Awesome! She wants me to move in with her but I'm about to pop that question to her first."

"Are you serious, Mookie?"

"As serious as a heart attack, Damien."

"I'm proud of you, man."

"But I'm more proud to have a good woman like Nadine having my back."

"Yeah, being that she even helped you secure the mentor job at the Boys and Girls Club right here in Decatur."

"Exactly."

"How's everything going at the job?"

"I love it, Damien. It's quite easy being a mentor to kids who look up to you especially with my story."

"Well, it's great you can give back and help others too."

"I'll be giving back even more this fall."

"What's going on then, Mookie?"

"I've been invited back for my second year as the strength and conditioning coach at my alma mater, Southwest Dekalb High School."

"Those young boys don't know they got their work cut out for them this fall."

"No doubt, Damien. Well, enough about me what's been going on with you?"

"I'm still trying to secure this one major account to

really get my marketing consulting business off the ground."

"And how are things going with the women?"

"I don't know what you mean when you say women, Mookie."

"Oh, now, you caught a slight case of amnesia, Mr. Ladies' Man."

"Now, don't you start with that again. If my memory serves me correct, you started the whole 'starting five' concept way back in college."

"Yeah, that's when I was young, dumb, and full of cum. In the end, it was all a bunch of nonsense."

"You can say that again."

"So you're basically now with Diamond, huh?"

"Pretty much so, bro. But I can't lie, I still think about Crystal and what could have been."

"Then maybe you should think about giving her a second chance."

"After what she did to me, Mookie, I don't think so."

"Everybody deserves some sort of second chance in life or love, Damien. Heck, look at me I'm a prime example."

Our conversation was becoming more in depth.

Before I could follow up with his last statement, Mrs. Wysinger appeared at the patio's entrance. She had a single plastic bag full of items in her hand.

"There you two are," she said looking at both of us. "Dinner will be ready in about one hour."

"Okay, Mrs. Wysinger," I said as Mookie simply smiled. "Just take your time."

After Mrs. Wysinger departed for the kitchen, Mookie and I continued to converse. But this time, Diamond and Crystal were not a part of it.

Within an hour, dinner was served just like Mrs. Wysinger promised. At the dinner table, we all talked about the good old days but now realized we were blessed to have each other. I was glad to have Mookie and his mom in my small circle. Throughout the evening and into the night one thing stood out. And that was how Mookie mentioned everyone deserves a second chance.

CHAPTER 9

It was nine o'clock in the morning as I lay in the bed with my eyes glazing at the white ceiling above me. I thought about Crystal and how much she meant to me now. Apparently, I still had some sort of feelings for her but my ego wouldn't allow me to move forward. Ever since that fall night about six months ago when I walked out of her home I still hadn't spoken with her. Now, don't get me wrong, she did call me plenty of times but just like the past I just blew her off.

For once and for all, I decided to put an end to this madness. I felt I at least needed to communicate with Crystal and tell her how I felt. And if I did still harbor any real feelings for Crystal I would know by speaking with her. While still looking up, I reached over to my nightstand for my cell phone. Once I had it in front of me, I looked aimlessly at the blank black screen. Suddenly, my phone rings and its Crystal's number.

"What the hell?" I shouted out loud to myself while looking at my phone. "Now that's some real déjà vu for you."

I accepted the call as I didn't want Crystal to have any second thoughts and hang up. After I said my customary hello, there was a short pause before she spoke.

"Hello Damien," said the soft voice on the other end. "It's me Crystal."

"Hi Crystal," I calmly answered back. "How are you?"

"I'm doing fine," she replied. "But I'm more concerned about you."

"Why is that?"

"Well, for starters you haven't answered any of my calls for months now."

"Yes, I know Crystal."

"And what was that all about the last time we were together, Damien?"

"I just had to leave."

"You rudely left me with no explanation."

"It's not as bad as you're making it out to be, Crystal."

"Damien, that's easy for you to say."

"I think we just need to talk."

"That's what I am calling you about. I'm free this afternoon if you want to meet for lunch."

"I figured a successful physician, with a thriving medical practice, would barely get to take time off during the week."

"Actually, I'm at the office now but have to meet with one of my patients at their home later today."

"Wow, you really go way out for your patients, Crystal."

"It's part of my duty and oath to be unconventional at times."

"Okay, so what time do you want to meet?"

"I'm here in the office until noon so let's meet at one o'clock."

"That works for me but where?"

"Let's meet at Atlantic Station again."

"How did I know you were going to say that?"

"Because you know me as much as I know you."

"I assume you want to meet at Fox Sports Grill like last time."

"No, let's shoot for Copeland's Cheesecake Bistro."

"That's an excellent choice, doctor."

"Okay, Damien, I'll see you later this afternoon."

"I'll see you then."

Somewhat satisfied, I jumped out of bed in order to really get my day started. The best way to do that was a good workout. Quickly, I washed my face, brushed my teeth, threw on my exercise apparel, and then headed for the door.

When I reached the gym on the second floor there were only a few people inside the facility. I kept my normal routine as I had done for so many years. First, I dedicated thirty-five minutes for cardio by running on the treadmill. After that, I hit the free weights for twenty-five minutes just to keep my body toned. Finally, I did my mandatory three hundred sit-ups and push-ups to complete my workout. To really cap it off, I ran up the stairs to my condo on the twelfth floor.

In the kitchen, I fixed myself an amino acid protein shake. Then I surfed the internet on my laptop for the latest news. When that was complete, I took a long hot shower and began getting ready to meet Crystal for lunch.

Moments before I arrived at the restaurant, Crystal texted me she was already seated. When I entered the nice establishment, I was quickly greeted by a female hostess.

"Hello, sir, will you be dining for one today?" she asked while standing behind a podium.

"I'm meeting someone who's already been seated," I answered. "I think I should be able to find her."

"Very well, sir," said the hostess. "Enjoy your meal."

"Thank you," I responded as I made my way into the dining area.

After walking a few paces, I quickly noticed Crystal sitting down at a nearby table. She sat there still looking petite and pretty. Her sandy-brown hair complemented her bronze-tone complexion. From what I could see, she was wearing a light grey business suit and ultimately noticed me once I reached the table.

"Well, there you are," she said as I walked up to her smiling. "Please have a seat."

"Yeah, I finally made it," I said reaching for my chair. Then I sat down. "Have you been here long?"

"No, I've only been sitting here for a few minutes."

"That's good I didn't want to have you waiting too long."

Suddenly, a male server appeared at our table and caught our attention. He welcomed me and then gave us our menus. After he took our drink order he suggested a few lunch specials. Then he allowed us to browse the menu while he retrieved our drinks.

"What do you have a taste for?" Crystal asked.

"I can't decide because everything looks great on the menu," I replied.

"You really can't go wrong with anything here, Damien," Crystal said.

"Yeah, you're probably right. I'll most likely get something simple yet fulfilling."

Soon our server was back at our table. Crystal selected the shrimp, crab, and avocado salad. I opted for the jambalaya pasta. After we made our selections, it was only a few moments before our server reappeared with our meal. We both dug in because everything tasted so great. Then our conversation began to get a little more serious.

"Damien, do you remember our last lunch date?" Crystal asked while fumbling her fork through her salad.

"Yes, I do," I replied after I wiped my mouth with my linen napkin.

"You never answered the question I asked you, Damien."

"What question was that, Crystal?"

"The one about whether you believe in fate or

destiny."

"I believe things happen and work out the way they're supposed to."

"How will things ever work out with us, Damien?"

"Crystal, I simply don't know."

"Baby, I still love you and want us to put our lives back together again," Crystal announced. "Will you give us a second chance?"

"I don't know, Crystal," I answered wiping my forehead with my linen napkin. By now I was sweating from the spicy meal and the heat Crystal was giving me.

"Well, when will you know, Damien?"

"Soon, Crystal, I promise."

I still loved Crystal with all my heart but my ego got in the way of telling her that right then. I even forgave her for what she did but still had a glimpse of indecisiveness of what to do next. Instead of continuing the conversation, I moved my chair back from the table.

"Where are you going, Damien?"

"I'm headed to the men's room and will be back in a minute."

In the restroom, I splashed some cold water on my face. Then I looked into the mirror at myself patting my face dry. When I regained my composure, I headed back to the table where Crystal was still seated. After I sat down, neither one of us said much of anything. Then our server reappeared to break the silence.

"Would you like some more water, sir?" he asked looking at my half-emptied glass.

"No thanks," I answered.

"But you can bring the check," said Crystal after I spoke. "I'll be paying the bill."

"Yes, ma'am, as you wish," he responded and hurried away.

Once Crystal took care of the bill we left the restaurant together. Outside, we gave each other a hug. I even told her about my upcoming business meeting with Jamison and his investor. After our brief small talk was over, we both went our separate ways.

CHAPTER 10

It was about a half hour after our lunch date and Crystal was almost at her destination. She drove her white Mercedes Benz S550 down Joseph E. Boone Boulevard which was also known as Simpson Street back in the day. She was in the Vine City section of Atlanta which was as very rough neighborhood.

The once prominent area where Dr. Martin Luther King, Jr. formally lived was very different now. Along the street Crystal traveled were abandoned boarded-up houses. Thriving businesses were now nothing more than deserted buildings and eye sores. Young boys, hanging out on the street corners, yelled at the luxury car but Crystal paid them no attention. She was focused on getting to her patient.

When Crystal finally reached the tiny house, she

pulled up and parked along the curb. Before she exited her sedan, she looked around and noticed hopelessness and despair. What she saw was similar to what she witnessed in South Central Los Angeles. Undeterred and without hesitation, she grabbed her large leather purse and headed to the house a few feet away.

"Mrs. Baptiste, it's Dr. Gayle, your physician from the medical practice," Crystal yelled out after she knocked on the door. There was still no results as Crystal continued to knock and patiently wait. "Mrs. Baptiste, are you in there?"

After what seemed to be an eternity, Crystal heard some movement in the small house. Someone from behind the other side of the door began to speak.

"Is that you out there, Dr. Gayle?" asked the voice.

"Yes, Mrs. Baptiste, it's me," answered Crystal.

"Well, I don't hear or see to good but you do sound familiar."

"Mrs. Baptiste, I can assure you I'm your physician."

"Okay, just give me a second to unbolt these locks on my door so I can let you in."

"It's no problem just take your time."

The elderly woman Crystal was speaking to through

the door was one of her patients, named Leila Baptiste. She was from Haitian descent and had lived in the Vine City area for almost sixty years. At almost ninety years old, she was still in adequate shape although she did have some health concerns.

"Yes, indeed, you are my doctor," said Mrs. Baptiste as she looked at Crystal after opening the door. "One thing I haven't lost is my memory. Come on in, child."

"How have you been, Mrs. Baptiste?" Crystal asked slowly walking into the quaint home.

"Oh, I guess about the same."

"Well, let me close the front door and I can get you situated."

Crystal closed and locked the front door behind her. Mrs. Baptiste stood there barely five feet tall and slightly slumped over waiting for further instructions. From the entrance, you could view the entire dwelling consisting of two bedrooms, the kitchen, a bathroom, and the living room.

"Dr. Gayle, you're still pretty like the last time I saw you," said Mrs. Baptiste adjusting the glasses on her face.

"Thank you, Mrs. Baptiste," Crystal exclaimed.

"Let's take a seat right here on the sofa."

"That's where I was seated before you knocked."

"Have you given some thought about what we talked about the last time you were in my office?"

"No, Dr. Gayle, I'm fine right here."

"But Mrs. Baptiste, I seriously think you should consider living in an environment with additional assistance for you."

"This is the only home I've known for so many years. I couldn't ever think about leaving it."

"I'm just afraid something may happen to you, Mrs. Baptiste."

"I'll be just fine," the elderly woman proudly announced. "Besides, my deceased husband bought this home when Vine City was a well-to-do neighborhood. Now, it's all I own."

"I understand," Crystal said diplomatically.

"Did you bring my medication like you promised?"

"Yes, ma'am, I did."

"Bless you, child. With my little monthly income, I can barely keep the lights on."

"Why don't you let me take your vital signs just to make sure you're fine?"

"Okay, whatever you say."

The pair continued to sit next to each other on the sofa as Crystal opened her large leather purse. She retrieved her stethoscope and portable blood-pressure kit.

"Now, I want you to take a deep breath when I place the end of this stethoscope on your back," Crystal ordered as she fitted the device within her ears.

"Yes, I understand," said Mrs. Baptiste.

And just like Crystal requested, Mrs. Baptiste followed her instructions during the brief exam. Then Crystal fitted the elderly woman's arm with the blood-pressure kit. Finally, Crystal did some additional test to make sure her patient was fine.

"Okay, Mrs. Baptiste, you're basically alright," Crystal said removing her medical instrument from her ears. "Your blood pressure is a bit high but the medication I brought should help control that."

"Will you fetch me a small glass of water from the kitchen?" Mrs. Baptiste humbly asked.

"Sure, that's no problem at all."

"The glasses are in the cabinet above the sink."

Crystal quickly went to the kitchen and found a small glass precisely where the elderly woman said it would be. She filled the glass with water and returned to the sofa. There she took a seat and handed the glass to her patient. Then, she retrieved the medication from her purse. Crystal sat silently as Mrs. Baptiste swallowed the pills and washed them down with the glass of water.

"How do you feel?" asked Crystal.

"Better so now we can move on," answered Mrs. Baptiste changing the subject. "Did you bring the item?"

"Yes, I did."

"What did you bring me?"

"It's a linen napkin he used while we had lunch today," Crystal answered pulling it from her purse.

"Yes, that's perfect," Mrs. Baptiste said smiling.

"Wait a minute Mrs. Baptiste. I really don't know about going through with all this."

"What do you mean, child?"

"It's so unorthodox and unreliable," Crystal said with hesitation. "I just see this as nonsense."

"Oh, there's no nonsense in the cards," said Mrs. Baptiste with confidence. "They have been predicting the future in my culture for generations. You do want to know the truth, right?"

"Yes, I guess."

"Then help me up and bring the linen napkin with us into the kitchen."

Crystal obeyed the elderly woman as if she was her

mother. When they arrived at the kitchen table, there were a set of tarot cards neatly stacked in the center. Crystal helped Mrs. Baptiste to her seat and then sat directly across from her. At the table, Mrs. Baptiste took possession of the linen napkin. She carefully opened it up fully and rubbed her hands throughout the item. Then she placed it to her nose and sniffed my scent. Finally, she neatly folded it and lightly brushed it along the top of the cards.

The elderly woman then took the tarot cards and shuffled them once. She laid them faced down in a row. There were four rows consisting of four cards in each row. Each card represented something specific such as death, fortune, the devil, a fool, the world, and most importantly the lovers.

"Now, child, select your one card but slowly and wisely," said Mrs. Baptiste in a serious tone.

"I'll select this one," Crystal said pointing to one card.

"Are you sure?"

"Yes, I am."

Mrs. Baptiste looked at the faced-down card Crystal had chosen. Then she picked up the card and turned it over on the table. Crystal looked at the card in amazement with her eyes and mouth wide open. She remained silent in disbelief and then looked at Mrs. Baptiste for an answer.

CHAPTER 11

It was a warm day in Atlanta but just another routine Saturday at Styles Salon. As always, the modern, sleek, and slick salon was filled with women attempting to look their best for the weekend. Of course, Raphael had the most clients waiting and kept the patrons entertained with his flamboyant personality.

Diamond, like most salon owners, was making sure the day-to-day operations were running smoothly. By now, her salon had a thriving clientele and she rarely worked on anyone. She preferred to rather just handle the business side of the operation.

Tameka stepped away from her desk momentarily. She was helping Diamond with inventory located, in the display case, near the front entrance.

"I'm so surprise how we're almost sold out of our eco-green shampoo and conditioner," Diamond said counting a few bottles left in the case. "Let's order another case from our sales rep. I'm sure he'll be happy to hear from us again."

"Yes, ma'am," said Tameka as she scribbled on the notepad she was holding. "I've added it to our list. Is there anything else?"

"Yes, just make sure you also order our usual necessary supplies for the salon. It's so busy in here now I'd hate to run out of something."

"Don't worry I have that covered already."

As Diamond continued to browse the display case, Tameka heard the phone ringing on her desk. Quickly, she removed herself from Diamond's side to answer the call.

"Styles Salon in Buckhead," Tameka said placing the receiver to her ear. "How may I assist you today?"

"Yes, ma'am, I'm trying to reach the owner of your establishment," said the caller.

"Sure, may I place you on hold for a moment?"

"Yes, that's fine."

Tameka repositioned herself back by Diamond who was still standing by the display case.

With her notepad still in hand, she addressed her boss.

"There's someone requesting to speak with you on the phone."

"I'll take it in my office, Tameka. What line is the caller on?"

"Um, line three."

"It's probably one of my new vendors calling me back from earlier this week. You can go ahead and place the supply order now. I think I have everything covered."

"Alright, I sure will."

Diamond made her way to the back of the salon. There she kept a decent-sized private office to handle any affairs. After entering the office, she closed the door. Then, she took a seat behind her mahogany desk and picked up on line three.

"Hello, how may I help you?"

"Well, for starters, you can stop avoiding me."

"Who is this?"

"You know good and goddamn well who this is!"

"Listen, I really don't have the time to talk with you right now."

"Oh really, Diamond. As serious as this matter is and you can't find time to speak with me."

"That's what I said."

"Well, then when?"

"I really don't know. I'm going to hang up now."

"Oh, no you don't."

"Yeah, then just watch me."

"I swear if you hang up this phone in my face again…"

"You'll do what?"

"I'll come down there and make a mockery out of you at your salon. Now, think about that before you react foolishly."

"Okay, what do you want?"

"Don't ask me that stupid ass question! Dammit, I want you to talk to me like you have some common sense about what's going on between us."

"Okay, I'm listening."

"Not over the phone but in person."

"You can't be serious."

"I'm very serious, Diamond. Meet me at the parking garage adjacent to Georgia Pacific building downtown. Drive to the upper deck where it's open, visible, and safe."

"When?"

"Be there in thirty minutes."

"The salon is real busy, right now, with it being

Saturday and all. I don't think I can meet you today."

"Your receptionist, Tameka, can handle any calls until you return. Stop stalling and get a move on."

Before Diamond had a chance to respond, the caller simply hung up. She grabbed her purse and made a dart for the front entrance of the salon.

"Tameka, I'll be back in a minute," Diamond said as she walked quickly past the receptionist's desk. "Don't call me on my cell phone if an issue comes up. I'll deal with it when I return."

"Okay," Tameka clearly said as she sat there. She looked a bit confused as Diamond headed out of the front door.

By the time Diamond whipped her BMW X5 in the upper deck of the parking garage, the person she was meeting was already there. The person was standing next to a Cadillac Escalade. She promptly pulled over to it. Before stepping out, she noticed there were no other cars on the upper deck. The sun was beaming on the concrete as there wasn't a cloud in the sky. Tall buildings surrounded the structure and made the view of the Atlanta skyline look picture perfect.

"Okay, I'm here just like you ordered," Diamond said as she got out of her vehicle.

"It's about time," said the person moving a bit closer to her.

"Why am I here?"

"Diamond, we need to get everything out in the open."

"I told you already I have everything all worked out. You're no longer needed."

"You think that's fair?"

"Life's not fair, that's just the way it is."

"I could give you so much more that's why I don't understand you."

"You and I were morally wrong from the beginning. I was young, naïve, and wasn't thinking straight."

"But I was wrong, too. We both know two wrongs don't make a right."

"So what are you saying?"

"At least let me have some input in your life."

"No, it's better this way."

"Damn, you're so cold, Diamond!"

"I told you already, life's not fair. Don't call me ever again. As far as I'm concerned this matter is closed."

Diamond, who was highly agitated by now, suddenly rushed into her SUV. She pressed the accelerator and made a fast dash for the exit ramp leading to the street level. The person she was speaking to was left there dejected, disappointed, and speechless. The only thing they could do was soak in the bright sunshine and look at the picture perfect Atlanta skyline.

CHAPTER 12

"Oh, Damien, I really don't want to see you go," Diamond said as we sat curbside in her vehicle at Hartsfield-Jackson Airport. "I'm going to miss you."

"C'mon, baby, we already discussed this," I said looking into her eyes. "I'll only be in L.A. for three days."

"Yeah, I guess I'm being selfish again."

"No, it just means you love me like you say you do."

"Well, say hello to your grandmother for me. I'm sure she can't wait to see you again."

"If I didn't make this trip she would really have a fit. I've only been back to L.A. twice since living in Atlanta all these years."

"Promise me you'll call me as soon as you arrive in L.A.," Diamond said moving forward to give me a kiss.

"I promise, baby," I said after our lips parted. "Are you going to be okay while I'm gone?"

"Don't worry about that, Damien. The salon is fully booked for the next few days. Plus I have a meeting with a new potential vendor."

"That's good just make sure you keep it tight for me until I return."

"It's all yours, baby, and nobody else. Don't you want me to pull into a secluded area of the parking garage and show you?"

"Damn, that sounds so enticing but I really have to be going now."

"I know, Damien, but I'll be sure to show you when you get back."

"You promise to give it to me just like the last time when I cooked for you?"

"Yes, but even better."

"Now you have me wanting to postpone my flight."

"Oh, no you don't, Damien," Diamond said with a grin. "Your grandmother is waiting for you."

"Okay, I hear you," I said reaching for the door handle. "I don't want to disappoint her. Oh, by the way, when I get back we have to meet with Mookie."

"Mookie."

"Yeah, you remember him don't you?"

"Yes, I do. I still remember the day when you called me about that terrible accident he had."

"Well, he's paid off his debt to society and is doing pretty good now."

"Oh really."

"Yes, Diamond, he has a steady job but most importantly a woman in his life now. He wants us all to meet for an outing."

"And do what?"

"Nothing too extravagant I assume. He probably just wants to meet for dinner or something."

"That sounds fun, Damien. We can make a double date night out of it."

"Yes, I figured that would be a good idea when he made the suggestion to me. Okay, baby, I really have to be going before I miss my flight."

"Be safe and I love you."

"I love you, too."

Diamond and I kissed one final time before I opened my door. I grabbed my single luggage bag from the rear. Then I watched her pull away from the curb and merge into the busy airport traffic.

Once inside the ever-busy airport, I checked my luggage. Then I went through the mandatory security check point and headed towards the terminal where my flight would depart. About three and a half hours later, I arrived at LAX. Promptly, I retrieved my luggage from baggage claim then called Diamond to let her know I had made it. Shortly, I located an Enterprise Rent-A-Car office inside the airport. Within minutes, I was in a mid-size sedan headed towards South Central L.A.

Nothing much had changed in the Crenshaw district as I traveled towards my grandmother's house. The overcast skies and the cool balmy weather were still consistent as well. Finally, I reached my destination and pulled into my grandmother's driveway at her house. Eagerly, I grabbed my luggage and her house key which I still had. Then I headed inside.

"Damien, is that you?" asked my grandmother as I came through the front door. She was meddling around in the kitchen.

"Yes, grandma, it's me," I proudly announced as I put my luggage down.

"Boy, if you don't get over here and give me a hug!" she ordered.

"How have you been, grandma?" I asked hugging her.

"I've been well, Damien. And how about yourself?"

"I'm doing pretty well myself."

"That's so good to hear and you look good, too. How was the flight into L.A.?"

"It was smooth sailing."

"Good. Now, take a seat at the kitchen table. You can join me for a fresh cup of hot tea."

"Okay."

I sat down at the table that had always been in my grandmother's kitchen for as long as I could remember. As I looked around, I noticed her quaint house was still clean and intact. She grabbed two tea cups from the cabinet and placed them on the table. Then she went to the stove and retrieved the hot tea. Slowly, she returned to the table and filled both cups. Afterwards, she placed the hot tea back on the stove. Before making her way back to the table, she grabbed two spoons and some sugar.

"Whew, now I'm ready to rest my old bones," she said sitting down at the table with me.

"C'mon, grandma, you're not old," I added as I put some sugar into my cup. Then I stirred the tea with my spoon.

"Well, I can't tell, Damien. I'm just waiting on the Lord to take me home. So how is your job with Coca Cola coming along?"

"Grandma, Coca Cola laid me off about a year ago."

"Why are you just now telling me that, Damien?"

"I just didn't want you to worry. Besides, I've been doing well for myself with my own marketing consulting business."

"Well, thank the Lord. I always knew you had an entrepreneurial spirit about you."

"Yes, I think it's finally paying off."

"Damien, when are you going to settle down and give me a few grandchildren? At some point, in life, you must start living in the word and not the world."

"I'm glad you brought that point up, grandma," I said reaching into my pants pocket. There, I retrieved a small picture of Christian and lay it on the table in front of her. "Doesn't he look like me?"

"Boy, this child doesn't have a bit of Hardy in him," she said holding the picture close to her face. "Believe me, I know a Hardy when I see one."

"Wait a minute, grandma. Maybe you should put on your glasses."

"Damien, my glasses are for reading. There's nothing wrong with my eyes while I'm looking at this picture. Who is this child?"

"Let me get back to you on that one, grandma," I said grabbing the picture from her hand. Then I stuffed it back into my pants pocket.

"Wait a minute," she said looking confused. "Why won't you tell me who that child is in the picture?"

"I'll answer that question for you later but right now I need to know something."

"Okay, what is it?"

"Can a man be in love with two women at the same time?"

My grandmother paused before she answered and then looked at me as if she saw a ghost. Then she placed the cup of tea to her lips and took a sip. She momentarily turned her head away from me then looked in my eyes and spoke.

"Damien, I hope you're not turning out to be the man your grandfather once was."

"Grandma, you know I don't remember anything about him. Only that he passed away when I was about five years old."

"Yes, that's right. You had been living with us for a

few years after your mother and father died in that awful car accident."

"What type of man was my grandfather?"

"He was a good man and provider. Unfortunately, he had one fatal flaw."

"What was that?"

"He was in love with two women at the same time. He claimed he loved me and his mistress across town."

"What!"

"Yes, Damien, it's true. One day when your grandfather was at his other woman's house, her husband came home unexpectedly. In a rage, the man shot them both dead and later turned the gun on himself."

"Oh my, God, why didn't you ever tell me this before?"

"Our family decided we would never discuss it again after the funeral. And besides, a young boy growing up to be a man didn't need to hear that."

"Why did you stay with my grandfather when you knew he was messing around?"

"Because that's what a good woman did back in those days, Damien. It's probably something you would never understand."

"You're probably right, grandma. I guess a lot has

changed since back in those days."

"Well, now I need for you to answer a question for me."

"Sure, what is it?"

"Are you now the man that your grandfather once was?"

I couldn't say a word although I wanted to. Instead, I quickly took a sip of tea from my cup. Then the both of us sat there in silence not knowing what to say next.

CHAPTER 13

The next day my grandmother awoke early and fixed a scrumptious breakfast. The meal included omelets, grits, sausage links, bacon, and toast. We both sat at the kitchen table while she watched me devour my meal as if I hadn't eaten in days. Surprisingly, she only ate a slice of toast while drinking her black coffee. We never discussed the conversation we had yesterday. It was as if it never occurred. After the meal, I gave my grandmother a kiss and headed out the front door. My agenda for the day included surprising Coach Frazier with an unannounced visit.

While driving to Crenshaw High School, I decided to stop at a local convenience store. Actually, it was the same convenience store I had frequent so many times during my high school years. When I walked inside, I noticed it was still Korean-owned and nothing much had changed. Quickly, I walked over to the cooler and pulled out a single lemon-lime Gatorade and made my way to the cashier. After paying for the item, I walked towards the entrance but not before I opened the small bottle of liquid refreshment. In two huge gulps, I nearly finished the entire bottle. Walking to my car, I noticed an older gentleman sitting on the curb where I had parked. He was dressed shabby and seemed like he hadn't shaved or showered in days.

"Hey, brother, can you spare a little change for a man down on his luck?" asked the man looking up at me.

"Sure, bro," I answered as I opened my hand. "Here's my last three dollars. It's all yours now."

"Oh thank you so much," he said. Then he reached for the dollar bills, I handed to him, while still sitting on the curb. "May God bless you."

"Yes, and may he bless you, too," I answered. Then I turned up the remaining contents of the Gatorade and tossed the empty bottle in a trash can the man was sitting near.

By the time I entered my car, there were a few more people exiting the store. The man quickly turned his attention to them seeking more change. I backed my car out of the parking space, then put it in drive, and was on my way.

When I finally made it to Crenshaw High it was almost eleven o'clock. The sun was beginning to trickle through the clouds. I could tell it was going to be warmer than yesterday. I made it inside the almost deserted school and into the administrative office. While there, a few teachers still remembered me and I gave hugs to them all. I told them I was looking for Coach Frazier and they pointed me to his office. With a good pace, I headed down the hall and found his office door slightly ajar.

"Coach Frazier, are you in there?" I asked opening the door more. Then I stuck my head into the small office.

"All-Star, is that you?" he answered while glancing up from his desk. He quickly stood up after he knew it was me. "Come over here and give your old baseball coach a hug."

Just like he instructed, I gave the man who meant so much to me a hug. He was like the father I never had. Since moving to Atlanta, we spoke on occasion but I failed to visit him until now. By now, he was slightly grey-haired and his stomach bulged out from his waist a bit.

"How have you been making it?"

"As best as I can, Damien. How long has it been?"

"Too long, Coach Frazier."

"How's your grandmother doing?"

"She is doing just fine."

"God bless her because she raised a boy into one helluva man on what she had to work with. But I'm sure you already knew that."

"Yeah, I realized that a long time ago. I definitely wouldn't be where I am today without her."

"Well, I'm so glad you decided to stop by your old high school while you were in town."

"I wanted to come by and see where it all started for me. Plus I figured you would be here teaching summer school or something."

"Actually, I just finished teaching my only class for the day. Before you came in, I was headed to the school's baseball field."

"Oh yeah for what?"

"Well, around this time every day, I help the returning seniors work on their technique for the upcoming school year. I just want them to be better prepared for their final baseball season here."

"I see you're still at it. You're helping these young kids fully develop and be their best."

"Yes, and that's in and outside the classroom. Why don't you join me on the baseball diamond and give a few pointers to the kids."

"I'll join you but I don't know if I'm qualified to coach like you."

"Sometimes it's just about inspiring others, Damien. These young kids would love to hear how you made it from Crenshaw High to USC. You can even tell them how you tried out for the Atlanta Braves."

"Okay, I see your point, Coach Frazier."

"Good now follow me."

As we walked through the halls on our way to the baseball field, I remembered all the great memories I had at Crenshaw High. Coach Frazier and I even stopped by the school's athletic trophy case. There he pointed out all the trophies I helped Crenshaw High earned in the city school district my junior and senior year. He even mentioned my senior year stats for record home runs, batting average, and stolen bases were never broken. After dwelling in the past for a moment, we finally made it to the baseball field. There we found a group of young boys anxiously waiting. They faced us as we stood behind home plate.

"Alright, everybody, listen up," Coach Frazier barked out. "This person standing next to me is Damien

Hardy. Damien is a former standout baseball player from Crenshaw High. He also went on to play baseball at USC."

"Hi guys," I said waving at the group.

"He's going to talk to you about what it takes to make it to the next level athletically and academically," Coach Frazier said sternly. "But before her speaks, I want everyone out on the field for warm-up drills."

"C'mon, Coach Frazier, do we have to?" asked a young boy from the front row. "You know we're already in tip top shape."

"Hell yeah I want you to, Thompson," Coach Frazier snapped back. "I don't care how good of a shape you think you're in, the competition is always one step ahead of you. If I say everyone participate in warm-up drills then that's what I want and with no complaining. Do I make myself clear?"

"Yes sir!" the group of young boys answered back.

"Okay, you know the routine," Coach Frazier said loudly. "Get out there on the field now!"

The group of boys followed Coach Frazier's command and lined up as usual for their warm-up drills. Coach oversaw the boys momentarily then he made his way back to me.

"I see you're still stern as ever."

"Damien, I have to be. These kids nowadays don't want to work for anything unlike back in your days."

"I just think it's a sign of the times. The kids now are just different."

"Well, they're going to be in for a rough ride if they think everything in life is just given to them. And I'll be damn if they think I won't make them work for it especially on my watch."

"Hey, I hear you loud and clear, Coach Frazier."

"Anyway, enough of that. How are things in Atlanta?"

"Everything is just fine."

"Have you settled down yet?"

"Not yet, Coach Frazier."

"Well, what are you waiting for, Damien? I heard there are a million beautiful black women in Atlanta. Surely, a guy like you should be able to settle down with one of them."

"I'm sure it will happen one day when it's supposed to."

"Yes, that's right, Damien, it always does."

Coach and I continued our talk while we watched the group of boys. He was absolutely right there were plenty of beautiful black women back in Atlanta. But at that moment, I only thought of two. One was Diamond and the other was Crystal.

CHAPTER14

As I was driving back to my grandmother's house, I thought about how good it was to see Coach Frazier again. Besides him being my high school baseball coach, he was a great mentor and father figure. Now, I give all the credit to my grandmother, who raised me, but he really kept me on the straight path especially during my adolescent years.

It was early afternoon and I figured my grandmother was preparing lunch. Just to be sure, I picked up my cell phone and decided to dial her home number. As I dialed the number, I received an incoming phone call from Raphael.

Now, as you should have remembered Raphael and I were first cousins. Our fathers were brothers and we both graduated from Crenshaw High back in '93. Back then and even now I never questioned his sexuality. I respected the fact he was just being who he really wanted to be.

"Hey boo boo!" Raphael said in an excited tone.

"What's up, cousin?" I said holding the cell phone to my ear while driving.

"I just spoke to grandma and she told me you were in L.A."

"Yeah, I came back home for a few days. I just had to tie up a few loose ends."

"What are you doing now?"

"I just visited with Coach Frazier at Crenshaw High."

"You mean fine ass Coach Frazier from back in the day?"

"Well, I don't know about all that, Raphael?"

"Oh, Damien, I ain't going to lie. When I used to come to your baseball games, all eyes were glued to Coach Frazier. I loved the way he maneuvered around the dugout with his fine self."

"Okay, Raphael, that's enough. You know that's way too much information for me."

"Don't shoot the messenger, Damien. I'm just telling the truth."

"What's going on in the ATL?"

"How the hell would I know? I'm actually in L.A. right now. And I'm mad you didn't let me know you were here too."

"C'mon, Raphael, how was I supposed to know you would be in L.A. the same time I was here?"

"Yeah, I see your point."

"What are you doing in L.A. anyway?"

"Honey, I'm here with one of my rich misses or should I say bitches doing her hair. She's here on business but wanted me to be her personal stylist for a few days."

"Wow, that must be nice. I assume she took care of your fees and expenses too."

"Boi stop! You know I wouldn't have it any other way."

"Where are you staying while you're in L.A.?"

"We're both at the Westin downtown."

"You mean the one on South Figueroa Street?"

"Yeah, that's the one. Why don't you meet me in the hotel bar for a drink?"

"You know I hardly ever drink. Besides, I'm headed back over to grandma's house to check on her."

"She's fine, Damien, I just spoke to her. As a matter of fact, I want you to meet my rich bitch I'm in town with."

"Okay, Raphael, let me call grandma just to be sure. If she's fine, I'll shoot down there but I'm not drinking anything."

"That's fine, Damien. We can just grab a bite to eat and it will be on me."

"Okay, cousin, I hope to see you soon."

"Chow baby."

After my conversation with Raphael ended, I placed a call to my grandmother. She had prepared fried pork chops smothered in gravy which was my favorite meal. Surprisingly, she encouraged me to meet with Raphael while he was in town. She also mentioned she would be fine as I could eat my meal later tonight.

When I arrived downtown, I quickly parked in the hotel's parking garage and made my way inside the establishment. There I passed the concierge's desk and was greeted with a smile by a woman. I found my way to the bar and noticed Raphael sitting down at a table. He was facing me but the woman sitting with him had her back towards me. As I approached the table, Raphael stood up and smiled.

"Damien, I'm glad you were able to drop by," Raphael said as I made it to his table.

"It's no problem at all, Raphael," I said looking at

his guest. "Katrina!"

"Well, hello there Damien Hardy," Katrina said then flaunted a devilish grin.

"Damien, please don't be mad at me," Raphael whispered into my ear. "She gave me an extra hundred dollars to get you here."

"I swear if you weren't my cousin," I whispered back.

"Why don't you have a seat?" Katrina insisted.

"Yes, Damien, take my seat," Raphael said. "I think I see an old flame at the bar ordering a drink and he's looking tasty. I'll let you two get reacquainted."

Raphael bolted away before I could utter another word. Reluctantly, I took a seat at the table and faced Katrina.

"Can I buy you a drink, Damien?"

"No thanks, Katrina, I'm fine."

"Are you sure? You look a little uptight."

"I'm positive. I'm fine."

"Well, suit yourself. I'll just enjoy my cosmopolitan all by myself."

"Let's cut to the chase, Katrina. What did you want to see me for?"

"I thought maybe we could familiarize ourselves

with one another while we're both in L.A."

"Really?"

"Yes, Damien, and I know things ended on a sour note the last time we were together. But I'm willing to let bygones be bygones."

"Well, seems like you and Raphael are doing pretty good with familiarizing yourselves with one another."

"Oh stop it, Damien. He couldn't fuck me if I gave him your big dick."

"But he's good enough to buy for all your dirty little tricks, huh?"

"Everyone can be bought, Damien. I see it every day in the courtroom."

"Not everyone, Katrina."

"So now you have morals? If I was a man propositioning you that would be fine, right? But you frown upon a power woman, like me, when the tables are turned."

"I'm simply just making a statement."

"Look, Damien, I just need a maintenance man I can call upon to fix me up every now and then. You know the kind that really knows how to stroke this wet pussy after I've had one too many cosmopolitans."

"Maybe this was just a bad idea for me to come here in the first place," I said attempting to stand up.

"Wait a minute, Damien," Katrina ordered. "Please sit down I want to give you something."

Katrina reached into her lap and placed a petite purse on the table. From inside, she retrieved a small white envelope and slid it to me. Then she took another sip of her cosmopolitan.

"What's this?" I asked taking possession of the envelope.

"Open it up and see," she answered.

I did just that and inside the envelope were five one hundred dollar bills. With a perplexed look I focused my attention back to Katrina.

"Didn't I just tell you everyone can't be bought?" I said sliding the envelope back to her.

"Damien, please it's not for that," she said moving the envelope back towards me. "I know you're an enterprising entrepreneur and all. I also know starting a new business can be rough as well. Consider it as a small gift from me."

"Okay, Katrina, thanks for the gift but I'm leaving now," I said standing up. Then I shoved the envelope into my pocket.

"By the way, there's one other item I have to mention," she said.

"Yeah, what's that?"

"I'll be in the hotel's penthouse suite if you change your mind about what we discussed earlier. I've already given the concierge your name for full access."

"Goodbye Katrina," I said as I began to turn around. "I'll see you later."

"If not here maybe back in Atlanta real soon," she responded while raising her drink. "Hopefully real soon, Damien."

I hurried through the hotel bar and saw Raphael on my way out. While sitting with his male friend, he happened to glance at me. He waved and I simply nodded my head. As I walked to my car, I thought about Katrina and what just occurred. I really needed the five hundred dollars but I wasn't going to let her know that. Besides, the five hundred dollars to me was more like five nickels to her. She would never miss it at all. The only problem I faced was that the money, I took, wouldn't come back and hurt me in the long run.

CHAPTER 15

My trip to L.A. had concluded and now I was back in Atlanta. I really enjoyed seeing my grandmother again and was thrilled to reconnect with Coach Frazier too. Even though Katrina was the last person I thought I'd ever see in L.A., my brief meeting with her wasn't that bad.

It was almost eight o'clock on a Saturday night as I had just departed my condo in Buckhead. My destination was Diamond's townhome in Sandy Springs. Tonight, we had decided to meet Mookie and Nadine for a simple, yet fun, night out. Everyone agreed to meet at Lucky Pins Bowling Alley near East Atlanta. Diamond, like me, was anxious to meet the woman who seemed to make Mookie's life so complete.

As I continued my drive northbound on GA 400, I thought about the conversation my grandmother and I had about Christian's picture. Even though my grandmother was elderly, she wasn't senile. She still was wise and wouldn't dare steer me wrong. I thought about mentioning our conversation to Diamond but maybe tonight wasn't the right time. Thus, I abandoned that thought all together by the time I reached her residence.

I parked outside the front door and made my way inside the home. Then I found Diamond still in her bedroom on the third floor of the plush townhome. She was standing in front of the mirror with a stack of clothes lying on the bed.

"I see you're not quite ready," I said entering the bedroom.

"I'm sorry, Damien," she said turning away from the mirror momentarily to glance at me. "I've tried on at least four outfits and I can't make up my mind on what to wear."

Diamond was dressed fashionably casual and looking good as well. She stood there wearing designer jeans which hugged and showed off her ass. Her contoured shirt revealed the rest of her assets. Her hair was styled to fit the occasion and she wore her patented four-inch Gucci heels which were new.

"Baby, you look fine to me."

"Are you sure, Damien?"

"Yes, I am. Although, I think the designer heels may be a little overkill. We're just going bowling."

"Well, I've only been bowling once in my entire life. If I remember correctly, we get bowling shoes once we get there."

"Yeah, that's right."

"Then these heels should be fine since I won't be actually bowling in them."

"Yes, Diamond, for argument's sake you're right. Now, let's get going so we won't be late."

"Okay, let me grab my purse."

Diamond found her purse on the bed which was next to the pile of designer clothes. I found my way back downstairs with her following slowly behind me. Walking in four-inch heels down a few flights of stairs can be challenging even for Diamond. Therefore, she definitely took her time. Finally, we jumped in my bimmer and headed to our destination.

When we arrived at the bowling alley it was precisely eight-thirty. Diamond and I made our way inside and quickly noticed Mookie and Nadine standing near the bowling lanes. Both of them were casually dressed and looked nice together. Nadine was quite an attractive woman as she stood next to Mookie. Suddenly, we approached the pair.

"There you two are," Mookie said smiling. I could tell he was glad to see us.

"What's up, Mookie," I said smiling back. We gave each other our customary brotherly handshake and hug. "I hope we're not late."

"Not at all, Damien"

"Okay cool."

"Well, let me introduce everyone," Mookie said as he turned to his date. "Nadine, this is my good friend, Damien. We met our freshman year in college."

"Hello, Damien," Nadine said as we both shook hands. "I've heard nothing but positive things about you."

"Likewise, Nadine," I said. "It's great to finally meet you."

"And this is Diamond," Mookie said as everyone turned towards her.

"Hi, Diamond," Nadine said shaking her hand as well. "Oh, girl, I just love those heels you're wearing."

"Thank you, Nadine," said Diamond. "You don't think they're a little bit too much though."

"Oh, no, Diamond. They look great with what you're wearing."

"Since we're speaking about shoes, let's all head over to the rental booth and grab our bowling shoes."

"That's a good idea, Darryl," Nadine said.

I looked at Mookie and cracked a simple smile and he knew why. He never let anyone call him by his real name besides his mother. Even way back in our college days, when we were roommates, I didn't have the luxury of calling him Darryl. I guess he really did love Nadine and I was fine with that.

"Yeah, Darryl, I'll even lead the way," I said poking fun at his name. He couldn't do anything but chuckle a bit.

"Now, I'm going to warn everyone I'm practically new at this," Diamond said as we all walked slowly. "I've only been bowling once before, so don't laugh if I throw a few gutter balls."

"Diamond, I'm in the same boat," Nadine said. Then the two women began to laugh. "When Darryl said we were going bowling, I told him I wouldn't have the slightest clue on what I would be doing."

"Don't you two women worry," Mookie said. "Damien and I bowled all the time when we were in college to pass the time. The both of us are pros and we're going to show you how it's done."

The four of us finally made it to the area for our bowling shoes. Once everyone received their designated shoes, I calmly made a suggestion.

"Why don't you ladies secure a bowling lane for us?" I asked. "We'll go over and get some beverages and nachos from the snack area. Plus you two can get more acquainted with each other."

"Okay, that sounds good," said Diamond as Nadine agreed. "We'll see you guys in a minute."

The two ladies walked away while Mookie and I headed in the opposite direction. While we walked towards the snack area, I commenced a conversation.

"Man, I'm really proud of you, Mookie," I said. "Nadine seems like a real good woman."

"She's practically the perfect woman for me, Damien," he stated. "I'm truly blessed to have her in my life."

"Yeah, and being that she helped secure that job for you, I'd agree she was a blessing."

"I'm glad you brought up my job because I have to tell you something."

"What's that?"

"We're having a small event at the Boys and Girls

Club. A handful of city businessmen are coming by to speak to the kids about being entrepreneurs. It's part of my mentorship program."

"That sounds interesting, Mookie."

"Damien, I thought about your new consulting business. Maybe you could come by and speak to the kids as well."

"Man, I would love to."

"Now, some of the speakers are going to make a little donation to the club. Considering you're just starting your business you can just donate your time. Since you graduated from college and started your own business, I'm sure the kids would love to hear your story."

"When is the event?"

"It's coming up real soon, Damien. I have the specifics on the paperwork at home. I'll give you a call with the full details."

"Alright cool. Just let me know."

"There's one other event I wanted you to come to."

"Which event is that, Mookie?"

"Damien, it's my Fourth of July birthday party this year. It's going to be a roar because I have a special surprise in store for everyone."

"Is your mom planning to cook all that great food

like she did before?"

"Man, you know it."

"Bro, then you can count me in."

By now Mookie and I had arrived at the snack area. After I placed our order, we only had to wait for a few minutes before it was ready. While walking back to meet the ladies, I had a great feeling. I was proud Mookie and I was such good friends and he had come full circle in his life. The date night with our women was sure to be a blast. Now, it was time for the pros to show the rookies how to really bowl.

PART III

BETRAYED AGAIN

CHAPTER 16

It was a Thursday afternoon and Nicole had the rest of the day off from Coca-Cola. She had an appointment at Styles Salon to get her weave tighten up. Now, it had been a while since she last visited the salon, but it probably was due to her hectic work schedule.

Today, she was dressed well as usual. She wore her mandatory corporate attire which included a navy blue pin-striped skirt and jacket. On her feet was a pair of Jimmy Choo designer heels any woman would drool over. Entering the salon, Tameka was the first person she encountered.

"Good afternoon, Mrs. Jones," Tameka said from her desk.

"Hello Tameka," Nicole responded. Then she slowly looked around the establishment. "How have you been?"

"I've been quite well and how about yourself?"

"Oh, I have been about the same."

"Well, I was surprised to see your name on the appointment log today, Mrs. Jones. We haven't seen you in a while."

"Yes, work keeps me busy but such is life."

"You're a few minutes early for your two-thirty appointment with Diamond. She is on a business call in her office right now, but I can walk you to her workstation."

"Thank you, Tameka."

Diamond had established herself as a real business woman by now. She rarely styled anyone's hair since she had a slew of professionals working for her. But occasionally, she worked on a handful of clients and Nicole was one of them. Nicole was one of Diamond's first customers when the salon first opened.

Tameka promptly rose out of her chair to aid Nicole. She led the way as Nicole quietly followed her. Diamond's workstation was closer to her office and away from the other stylists. This gave her clients a sense of privacy. Moreover, they felt as if they were being pampered.

"Here we are, Mrs. Jones," Tameka said as the two reached their destination. "You can just have a seat in Diamond's workstation chair."

"I love this chair it's so comfortable," Nicole said taking a seat.

"Mrs. Jones, I just love those heels you're wearing." Tameka said looking down at Nicole's feet. "They are so gorgeous."

"You really like them?" Nicole asked.

"Yes, I do."

"Well, my husband gave them to me as a surprise a few days ago."

"I wish I had a man that would surprise me with a new pair of heels like those you're wearing."

"Be careful what you wish for, Tameka."

"Why do you say that, Mrs. Jones?"

"Because usually when a man surprises you with lavish gifts he's done something wrong."

"Okay, I'll be sure to remember that one."

"Yes, Tameka, be sure you do."

"Now, just sit here and relax. I'll let Diamond know you're in her chair waiting."

"Thank you, dear."

Nicole sat there patiently after Tameka had walked away. Nearby, she could hear the other stylists working on their clients. Most of them were chatting about the latest gossip, in Atlanta, like who was sleeping with whom. The chair Nicole was sitting in was surrounded by mirrors. While she waited, she looked at her hair and noticed it was still intact. After five minutes had elapsed, Diamond suddenly appeared.

"Girl, how have you been doing?" Diamond asked.

"Hey, Diamond," replied Nicole. "I've been busy working on a special project."

"Well, stand up and give me a hug," Diamond suggested.

"Oh sure," Nicole said rising out of her chair.

The two beautiful women embraced in a friendly hug. Then Nicole took her seat again while Diamond stood in front of her.

"I was surprised to hear you scheduled an appointment with me," Diamond said. "I haven't seen you since I first opened my salon over a year ago."

"Has it been that long ago, Diamond?" Nicole asked very seriously.

"Yes, I'm pretty sure, Nicole."

"Well, you know I've been busy with Coca-Cola

and all."

"They have you working hard over there, huh?"

"Yeah, but nothing this superwoman can't handle. I really love my job and don't mind all the extra hours."

"Nicole, sometimes you have to slow down and smell the roses before they wither away. And besides you should come in here and see me more often."

"I don't think Coca-Cola is going to let me slow down anytime soon, Diamond. We can compromise on me coming in here more often. I've seen what you've done with the salon and it really looks great."

"Thank you so much, girl. I've put my entire life into this salon and now we have fourteen full-time stylists plus business is booming."

"Since your salon is doing so well, would you be interested in how your business can make even more money?"

"I sure am. What did you have in mind?"

"Well, Diamond, I know of an individual looking to invest in start-up businesses here in Atlanta. I think your salon would be a perfect fit for what they're looking for?"

"How so Nicole?"

"For starters, your salon could be a great opportunity for franchising. You have an excellent brand, client base, and room for growth. Franchising your business would become an instant cash cow for you."

"Wow, that thought never occurred to me."

"I think it would be a perfect fit for your salon. But even if you didn't do that, you could allow the individual to invest capital into your business. Then take the proceeds and open up additional salons right here in Atlanta."

"That sounds impressive, Nicole. Now, what type of work are you in again?"

"I'm a marketing director for Coca-Cola. Occasionally, I meet global investors looking for the next big opportunity. And with this particular investor, I had you in mind."

"I'm grateful you would even consider me. So how do I get to meet this investor?"

"Don't worry I've taken care of that already," Nicole said as she reached into her purse. "Here's my business card. On the back you'll find the date, time, and location for the meeting."

"Okay," Diamond said as she took the card.

"I know you're a very busy woman just like me, Diamond. Once you checked your schedule let me know if the date and time doesn't work for you. I'll set up a new appointment."

"I should be able to make it, but if not I'll let you know."

"That's good to hear. There's just one other thing I have to mention."

"What's that's, Nicole?"

"If you don't mind, I'd like to sit in on the first meeting. I could act as the liaison and help break the ice."

"I don't see anything wrong with that. Actually, I would prefer if you were there for the initial meeting."

"The initial meeting shouldn't be too much of a hassle. I'll introduce you two and you can somewhat get a feel for one another before moving forward."

"I'm excited and can't wait to meet this investor. Now, that we've got that out the way, let's get down to some real business."

"And what might that be, Diamond?"

"Your hair."

The two woman laughed as Nicole almost forgot what she was really there for. Nicole explained what hair style she wanted. Then Diamond went to work on making her look more beautiful than she already was.

CHAPTER 17

Around four-thirty that same afternoon I decided to pop in at Styles Salon and surprise Diamond. Thank goodness Nicole had departed fifteen minutes earlier. I was in no way or form ready to ever deal with her crazy ass again.

As I entered the front entrance, I knew I had to deal with someone almost as bitter as Nicole. Tameka was standing up by her desk and kept her eyes glued on me until I reached her.

"Well, well, well look what the cat drug in today," Tameka said. She continued to look at me with a hateful stare. Then she eyeballed me from head to toe.

"I see you're in a better mood to see me this time

around," I said sarcastically.

"Oh, give it a rest, Damien. You're not all that anyway."

"I guess I'm not ever since I refused to taste your sweet potato pie, huh?"

"I can't help it if your girlfriend has your tired ass pussy whipped."

"Please, Tameka, you have nothing to offer but a big butt and pretty smile. Besides, I don't want what every man in Atlanta has had already."

"Forget you, Damien!"

"No, I think I'll forget all about how you tried to press up on me a few months ago."

"You really think you're all that? If your foolish ass only knew you would have tasted my sweet potato pie a long time ago."

"If I only knew what, Tameka?"

"If you only knew that…"

"Damien, what are you doing here?" Diamond asked as she suddenly appeared from the lounge area.

"Hey, baby, I thought I'd drop by and surprise you," I answered. "But it seems like you beat me to it."

"Oh, that was so sweet of you, Damien," Diamond said and smiled.

"Anything for you, Diamond," I exclaimed. Then I kissed the woman I loved so much.

"What were you two talking about before I walked up?" Diamond asked. "It seemed like your conversation was pretty in depth."

"Actually, Tameka was getting ready to tell me something she thought I needed to know," I said. "Right Tameka?"

"Never mind, Damien," Tameka said as she took a seat at her desk. "It really wasn't that important." Then she began to finagle with the computer, on her desk, as if she didn't want to be bothered.

"Okay, if you say so," I responded. Then I turned my attention back to Diamond. "Baby, let's get out of here. I want you and me to do something romantic."

"You mean I have the pleasure of being courted by Mr. Hardy?"

"Yes, baby, you do."

"And what might that entail?"

"I figured we would take a nice romantic evening walk, while holding hands, through Piedmont Park. We could further discuss our future and even watch the sun set among the city's skyline."

"Now, how could I refuse that? Let me tell my staff

I'll be leaving early. Then I'll grab my purse from the office and will be right back."

"Take your time, baby."

Diamond hurried away and I turned my attention back to Tameka. She kept her eyes fixed on the computer's monitor without looking at me.

"You know what I think, Tameka?" I asked.

"I'm pretty sure you're going to tell me, Damien," she said finally looking at me.

"I think you're jealous."

"Jealous of what?"

"That you're sitting behind this reception desk while you wish you could be running the show like Diamond. That's why you want to come between us so bad, right?"

"I know you think Diamond is all shiny and glittery, but don't be mistaken one day and come up with fool's gold."

Then Diamond walks up to the desk again before I could address Tameka's nasty remark. She had her designer purse in tow and was ready to go.

"C'mon, Romeo, let's go for our romantic walk," Diamond said. I'm all ready for you."

"Okay," I said. "I'll lead the way."

"By the way, Tameka, make sure you forward all my calls to voicemail," Diamond said. "And after you close up tonight, email me the final sales total for the day."

"Yes, ma'am, I sure will," was Tameka simple response.

We hardly made it to the front door when Raphael approached us. I really couldn't tell if he was in a good mood or not.

"Hey boo boo!" he lightly shouted.

"What's up, cousin?" I said.

"I know you weren't coming up in here and not even going to speak to your own cousin. I saw you leaving and had to break away from my client for a second."

"Raphael, I was just in here to pick up Diamond. I really didn't want to bother you since you were with someone."

"Well, where are you two headed if you don't mind me asking?"

"Just for an evening stroll in Piedmont Park," Diamond interjected. "Now, I believe your client needs your attention again."

"Oh, so Mr. Ladies' Man has turned romantic all of a sudden," Raphael jokingly said.

"Man, you know I never was a ladies' man," I

announced.

"Well, I'm glad someone around here finally found a good man," Raphael said to Diamond. "I can't wait until I find Mr. Right and I really do mean Mister Right. You two have fun and I'll see you tomorrow, Diamond."

"Okay, Raphael," she said laughing lightly.

The drive to Piedmont Park took less than ten minutes. I was surprised the traffic was so light and we were able to find a parking spot near the park. We both exited my vehicle and thus began our journey. The weather was warm as we noticed people walking their dogs, joggers, and others laying in the grass soaking up the sun. As we walked, holding hands, we came upon an ice cream vendor in the park. He had a small stationary cart and seemed to be in a pleasant mood.

"Sir, would you care to buy the pretty lady you're with an ice cream cone?" he asked.

"Yeah, I guess I will," I replied and then looked at Diamond.

"C'mon, Damien, you know I'm trying to watch my figure," she stated.

"Oh, baby, you're still going to look fine even if you only have one scoop."

"Okay, I guess I can cheat a little just this time."

"What flavor would you like, sir?" asked the vendor.

"We'll take two French vanilla scoops," I answered.

"Would you like those on a sugar cone?"

"Yes, that will be fine."

The man carefully picked up a sugar cone from his cart and placed one French vanilla scoop on top of it. Then he handed it to Diamond. Next, he repeated the process and gave me my ice cream cone.

"There you are, sir. That will only be eight dollars."

"Here's a ten, you can just keep the change."

"Much oblige to you, sir. I hope you and the pretty lady enjoy your ice cream as you walk through the park."

"Thank you, Mister, we will."

We both licked our ice cream cones as we walked without saying a word. The French vanilla flavor was delicious. I could tell even Diamond was glad she gave into her temptation.

"How was your trip to L.A.?" she said breaking the silence. "You really didn't say too much about it when you came back."

"It was a good trip, Diamond," I replied. "My grandmother and I were able to catch up on a lot of things."

"I'm so glad you went to visit her, Damien."

"I am too. It was good to get away and clear my head plus get a sense of clarity."

"As busy as I am, with the salon lately, I wish I could do the same."

"I'm not trying to get off the beaten path, Diamond, but let me ask you a question."

"Sure, Damien, go right ahead."

"Do you really love me as you say you do?"

"Yes, I really do love you. Now, where is all of this coming from, Damien?"

"Nowhere in particular, Diamond. I just wanted to hear that from you."

"Damien, I love you wholeheartedly. You can always trust and believe in that."

"That's good to know, baby. I love you, too."

We continued our trek throughout Piedmont Park licking on our ice cream cones until they were all gone. We spent the rest of the evening talking about our future with anticipated happy times to come. After we watched the sun set, I suggested we go back to Diamond's place. There, I would surprise her even more and lick on something else that was definitely tasty.

CHAPTER 18

Tomorrow was the big day and I was overwhelmed with excitement. My meeting with Jamison White and his investor was to take place. Now, I was mentally prepared and was eager to explain my proposal again if needed. On the other hand, I had to definitely look the part in order to impress. Therefore, I decided to visit the Macys at Perimeter Mall and purchase a new suit. When I arrived at my destination, it was only eleven o'clock in the morning and I was eager to shop. I quickly found my way to the men's department and browsed through the large section of suits.

"Good morning, sir," said a well-dressed man in a suit as he approached me.

"Good morning," I simply said.

"My name is Bernard and I'll be more than happy to assist you today."

"With all the suits you have here I'll probably need your help, Bernard."

"Well, what's the occasion for the suit you're shopping for?"

"It's actually for a business meeting with a client."

"I can show you an assortment of suits that I believe you'll approve. Would you prefer a European cut or a traditional suit?"

"What's the difference, Bernard?"

"A European-cut suit is more stylish and contoured to fit your body, while a traditional suit has less flair and fits conservatively."

"I don't want to look too flashy, Bernard. But I don't want to come across as being plain either."

"Sir, I would suggest a European-cut suit for your business meeting. The styles we offer are not too flashy and I believe you'll love the contemporary look."

"Okay, since you're the expert I'll go with what you suggest."

"That sound great, sir, just follow me."

I followed Bernard throughout additional sections

149

of the men's department. There, he showed me even more suits that were available. With men suits the color scheme is pretty simple. Your primary colors are navy blue, black, and gray. You could also have the luxury of selecting pin-stripes for the same colors as well. I finally picked out a charcoal-gray European-cut suit. The color was traditional but the style was contemporary. I knew I could turn a few heads once I had it on. Even Bernard was impressed by my selection.

"I believe I'll go with this one," I announced as I held the suit between us.

"Very nice selection, sir," he commented. "I see you have an excellent taste in clothes."

"I sure hope so, Bernard. I'll only get one chance to make a good impression with my choice."

"Don't worry about anything. I'll make sure we have your suit looking great on you. We'll need to have your suit tailored-fitted, when do you actually need the suit?"

"I need it by tomorrow afternoon. Will that be a problem?"

"No, sir, that won't be a problem at all. I can have our seamstress take your measurements now and have your suit ready by this evening."

"That sounds great."

" Let's get you to our dressing room where you can try on that suit. In the meantime, I'll call the seamstress up to take your measurements."

With the suit I proudly selected, I continued to follow Bernard throughout the men's department. We finally ended up where the dressing rooms were located. There, I tried on my suit and was even surprised more by how well it looked on me. Within a few minutes, the seamstress arrived and took all the required measurements for my inseam, waist, and jacket. Once that task was completed, I took off the suit and placed my clothes back on. As I exited the dressing room, Bernard was patiently waiting for me.

"Here you are, Bernard," I said as I handed him the suit on the hanger.

"Thank you, sir," he said. "Now, if you will continue to follow me, I'll take care of everything. Oh, by the way, will you need a shirt and tie to go along with your suit?"

"I might as well since I'm here."

"I'll take care of that for you also, sir."

I followed Bernard through the aisle where we ended up in a large section of dress shirts and ties. He used his expertise to find me a French-cuff shirt, tie, and even cufflinks to go with my suit. After that, we headed over to his register. There, he secured my pertinent information for having my suit tailored-fitted. Then, I gladly paid for all the items and was almost on my way.

"Sir, our seamstress will have your suit ready by six o'clock this evening. Will that be okay with you?"

"Yes, that's fine with me."

"When you come back this evening, we'll have you retry on the suit again. If something needs amending, we will have time to correct and adjust."

"Okay, Bernard, I'll see you later this evening."

"We look forward to serving you then. Enjoy the rest of your day, sir, and once again thanks for shopping at Macys."

As I left Bernard's register, I really had a good feeling. I was actually going to look as sharp as a tack as my grandmother would say. Before I left the store completely, I stopped in the men's shoes department and purchased a new pair of black leather loafers. Now, my ensemble was complete.

I spent the rest of the day running a few errands, making a few sales calls, and even getting a light workout in. By now, I was stretched out on my sofa listening to some relaxing music when my cell phone rang. I quickly jumped up and turned the music down as I answered the phone.

"Hello," I said.

"Yes, I'm trying to reach Damien," the caller announced.

"I'm Damien."

"Hi, Damien, this is Courtney. I'm just calling to let you know your results are in."

"That's good to hear, Courtney. What's the prognosis?"

"I'm sorry, Damien, I can't give out that information over the phone. You'll have to come by the office."

"Okay," I said looking at my watch. "What time do you close today?"

"We're here until five o'clock," she replied.

"I'll be there shortly."

"We'll see you then, Damien."

It was only a quarter after four when I hung up the phone with Courtney. Even though the office building was minutes away, I quickly headed out the door. It had been weeks since I last met with her and I was beyond anxious for the results.

When I arrived at the office it was only a few minutes before they closed. Thanks to the bottleneck traffic on Peachtree Road, I almost didn't make it there on time. Once inside, Courtney greeted me from behind the glass partition. She simply gave me a medium-sized manila envelope and thanked me for using their services. I took the envelope and went back to my car located in the parking lot. After taking a deep breath, I ripped open the envelope. As I read the report, I was flabbergasted but I shouldn't have been. I didn't want the details of the report to ruin my day. Additionally, I needed to refocus because tomorrow was a big day I couldn't blow. I started my car and put it in drive. Then I pressed the gas pedal and headed back to Macys to pick up my tailored-fitted suit.

CHAPTER 19

"Are you on your way right now?" Crystal asked.

"Yes, Crystal," I answered. I kept one hand on the steering wheel and the other on my cell phone, which was to my ear. "I'm actually on Peachtree Road and only a few minutes from the restaurant."

"Well, I just had a break from seeing a patient and thought I'd give you a call."

"That really means a lot, Crystal. I kind of thought you would have forgotten about my meeting."

"Damien, I would never forget something that was so important to you. And besides, I just wanted to call and say good luck."

"I'm going to need more than good luck to close

this deal. I just hope this investor sees me eye to eye on what I have to present."

"Don't start worrying now, Damien, you'll do just fine. You're ambitious, smart, and confident. Plus you know what you're talking about."

"I'm all of that rolled into one, huh? I like how it sounds. Maybe you should repeat that again for me."

"Don't press your luck, Damien."

"Well, Crystal, if all else fails maybe the new suit and shoes I bought will help seal the deal."

"Maybe so but I believe your presentation skills will be good enough. Don't worry and just be you."

"That's easy for you to say not to worry, Crystal. I've put so much time and effort into finalizing this deal. This one account could really get my business off the ground."

"Just keep thinking positive thoughts and everything will be okay."

"Alright, I will. Hey, I'm coming up on the restaurant now. So I'll talk with you later."

"Why don't you give me a call after your meeting? I'm anxious to hear how everything worked out."

"Yeah, that shouldn't be a problem."

"Maybe you can come over afterwards and we can

celebrate with a bottle of champagne."

"I like your wishful thinking, Crystal, and the champagne sounds nice too."

"I'll let you go now, Damien, they're paging me again. You'll do great and once again good luck."

"Thanks, Crystal, I'll talk with you soon."

As I pulled up to the entrance of the restaurant, I hung up my cell phone and stuffed it into my jacket. There were a few cars ahead of me and I glanced at my watch. It was fifteen minutes until two o'clock so I still had time to spare. Finally, the cars ahead of me moved forward and I approached a waiting valet. When I reached him, he opened my door.

"Welcome to Prime Restaurant, sir," said the valet. "I'll be more than happy to take your vehicle from here."

"Sure, just let me make sure I have everything before I get out," I said. Then I grabbed my leather portfolio from the passenger's seat. As I exited my car, the valet handed me a ticket stub.

"Here you are, sir," he said. "Just make sure you give one of the valets your ticket once you're ready to depart."

"Okay, I will," I announced as I took the ticket.

"Enjoy your meal, sir, and by the way nice suit."

"Thanks for the complement."

I walked towards the entrance as the valet whizzed off in my vehicle. As I entered the plush establishment, I was greeted by a female hostess. She was well dressed and stood behind a tall object shaped like a podium but wide like a desk.

"Hello, sir," said the hostess. "How may I help you today?"

"I'm scheduled to meet someone here for lunch," I replied. "He's probably already seated."

"Well, I can check for you, sir. What's the person's name you are meeting with?"

"His name is Jamison White."

The hostess turned her attention to the sheets of paper in front on her. She glanced over them thoroughly and then looked up at me.

"Sir, are you Damien Hardy?"

"Yes, I am."

"Sir, if you can just bear with me for a few seconds, I'll have someone take you to your party's table."

"Okay."

I stood next to the hostess as she picked up the receiver to the telephone that was near her. Quickly, she dialed a number and whispered to whomever she was speaking to. After her brief conversation was over, she hung up the receiver and continued to smile at me. Within seconds, a tall man wearing a suit approached me.

"Mr. Hardy, it's a pleasure to meet you," he said shaking my hand. "I'm Bret Caldwell the manager for this establishment. How are you doing this afternoon?"

"I'm doing well," I simply said.

"That's great to hear, sir. Now, if you can just follow me I'll lead you to your party."

"Alright lead the way and I'll follow."

Bret led me through the crowded dining room area. There were an abundance of people within the fine venue. As he maneuvered us through what seemed to be a maze of tables topped with white linen, I noticed we were headed to the middle of the dining room. I saw two figures in the distance but couldn't make out their distinction yet. I tried to remain calm and didn't want to be over zealous for my presentation. The closer we got to the table, the more I thought my eyes were playing tricks on me. Then my heart literally sunk into my stomach as I couldn't believe what I was seeing. At the large round table, Nicole sat on one side and Diamond was seated directly across from her. The two women were chatting and seemed to be in a good mood. Finally, Bret and I arrived at our destination.

"As you ordered, Mrs. Jones, I've brought Mr. Hardy to you once he arrived," Bret said looking at Nicole.

"Thank you so much, Bret," Nicole said. "I knew I could count on you. That will be all for now." Then Bret quickly hurried off as Diamond immediately spoke up.

"Damien, what are you doing here?" she asked with a perplexed look.

"I want to ask you the same question, Diamond," I replied. "But I think I already know the answer. It seems like we both have been duped."

"What is he talking about, Nicole?" Diamond suddenly asked.

"Well, let's not jump the gun just yet," Nicole answered. "Damien, why don't you please have a seat?"

"There's no way I plan to be a part of your wicked shenanigans again," I proudly said. "I'm out of here and I suggest you leave with me too, Diamond."

"Dammitt, I said sit your ass down!" Nicole exclaimed. She had raised her voice and struck her hand on the table while making the statement. A few patrons looked around to ensure everything was alright. "I swear if you don't I'll cause a scene in here you'll live to regret for the rest of your life."

"Baby, just have a seat," Diamond insisted. "I'm

curious to hear why Nicole brought all three of us here today."

"That makes two of us, Diamond," I said taking a seat. "Okay, Nicole, you got what you wanted. Now the floor is yours, let's hear what you have to say."

We all three sat there momentarily in silence. I looked at Nicole while she had a sinister look on her face. It was something I never wanted to see. And just like Diamond, I was curious to hear what she had to say.

CHAPTER 20

Before Nicole could say anything, a female server approached our table. She carried a tray on her shoulder and a plate sat on top of it.

"Here's one T-bone steak, medium rare, with a loaded baked potato for you, sir," she said. Then she placed the plate on the table in front of me.

"Wait a minute," I said looking at her as she walked away. "I didn't order anything."

"I ordered the meal for you, Damien," Nicole interjected. "Since you haven't tasted me in a while, I thought you might as well taste one of your favorite meals instead."

"Now, hold on for a second, Nicole!" Diamond

angrily yelled out. "How dare you disrespect me like that?"

"Girl, are you serious?" Nicole yelled back. "I haven't even attempted to tell Damien how disrespectful your sheisty ass is!"

"Who the hell are you calling sheisty you tramp?" Diamond fired back.

"Well, I rather be a high-end tramp any day than someone's whore," Nicole answered.

"I'll be damn if I sit here and listen to the both of you argue like two second graders," I blurted out. By now, even more patrons were turning around to witness all the commotion. When they realize everything was okay, they went back to enjoying their meals. "Now, Nicole, tell me what happened to Jamison White and why isn't he here?"

"Oh, Damien, how can you be so naïve for someone so smart?" Nicole asked. "Jamison White never existed. He was merely an actor I hired from a talent agency here in Atlanta."

"So the whole idea of him wanting to utilize my consulting business was just a scam, huh?" I asked.

"Yeah, pretty much so," Nicole replied. "I had to find a way to get you here without ruining the big surprise."

"Don't feel bad, Damien," said Diamond. "Apparently, she connived me into thinking there was someone who wanted to invest in my salon."

"Who's conniving who, Diamond?" asked Nicole as she focused on Diamond. "Do you really know who I am?"

"As far as I know your some delusional woman who came into my salon over a year ago," Diamond answered. "I should have never befriended you let alone styled your hair."

"Oh, you've known me for longer than that short time frame," said Nicole. "I knew of you when you danced at the Gold Club while you attended Spelman College."

"You must have fell and bump your head, Nicole," said Diamond. "I don't ever recall you working at the Gold Club."

"Girl, you really must be stupid," Nicole responded back. "I'm too smart and sophisticated to ever get on stage and shake my ass for money. But you didn't have a problem of shaking yours and enticing my husband."

"Your husband?" asked Diamond looking confused.

"Yeah, whore, my husband Maurice," snapped back Nicole. "The man you fucked over ten years ago, around the same time you were doing Damien. The same man who got you pregnant, but you had the gall to tell Damien he was the father."

"Damien, I know you don't believe this nonsense

Nicole is saying," said Diamond. Then she looked at me as if I was going to defend her.

"You're calling it nonsense, huh?" Nicole asked. "Well, I'm not done yet because there's plenty more."

"Let's here the rest, Nicole," I added as Diamond looked dejected.

"As you know, after Diamond graduated from Spelman, she quickly returned to Chicago," added Nicole. "But being a few months pregnant, by a married man, wouldn't sit too well with her parents. So she lied and told them she had a fling with you Damien but you disappeared."

"Keep talking, Nicole, I'm listening," I said.

"Maurice took several flights to Chicago after the child was born and met with Diamond secretly," Nicole stated. "He was more than generous and she loved his money. She knew he was the only one who could elevate her to where she wanted to be in life."

"Damien, her story isn't connecting at the dots," interrupted Diamond. "I know you're not going to continue to sit here and listen to this."

"Go ahead and continue, Nicole," I said.

"Maurice begged her to move to Atlanta where he could be closer to his son," continued Nicole. "After many years, she finally agreed but only if he financed the salon she always dreamed of having. I knew I should have beaten that bitch ass the first day I walked into her salon."

"I wished you would have tried!" said Diamond firing off at Nicole.

"But instead of doing that, Damien, I did something even better," said Nicole smiling.

"What was that?" I asked.

"I got even," she quickly answered. "When you told me about your high-end shoe hustle, I mentioned Diamond's salon to you. I knew once she saw you, she would conjure up a story about Christian being your son. She wanted her own husband to go along with her thriving business."

"So you pretty much were the mastermind behind the majority of all these events?" I asked.

"Your damn right I was," Nicole answered proudly. "I wanted Diamond's bubble to get a big as it could. Then I could come in and pop it. I figured that would be more satisfying than whipping her ass."

"Damien, that entire story is a lie," Diamond softly shouted. "Christian is your son."

"Christian isn't your son, Damien," Nicole responded. "She taught him everything about you at an early age hoping fate would one day intervene. The DNA test Maurice took a long time ago proved he is the father."

"What do you have to say for yourself, Diamond?" I asked. She sat there motionless as if she was thinking of how to respond.

"What's the matter, whore, cat got your tongue?" asked Nicole.

"Baby, I love you," Diamond finally said to me. "You know I would never intentionally do anything to hurt you. I just want us to be together forever."

"Yeah, I figured that out, Diamond," I said. "That's why I did my own investigation."

"What are you talking about, Damien?" asked Diamond.

"Remember the day we took Christian to the airport?"

"Yes, I do."

"Well, I took some hair from his brush and also gathered your hair earlier. Then I submitted those samples, along with my hair, to a DNA lab here in Atlanta. It turns out that Christian is not my son."

"Bravo, Mr. Hardy!" Nicole exclaimed as she clapped her hands. "I see you are still quite the intelligent man after all."

By now, Diamond retreated from any further arguments. She clearly had been made and tears began to flow down her pretty face. Calmly, she buried her face into her hands to hide the guilt and shame. Nicole and I sat there speechless.

"Oh, Damien, I'm so sorry," Diamond finally said as she looked up. Tears were still flowing as she picked up a linen napkin to wipe her face. "I just wanted the best for Christian."

Diamond stood up with the linen napkin still patting her face. She looked at me once again and quickly departed our table. The crowd noticed something was wrong as Diamond ran towards the entrance. Nicole sat there with the biggest grin on her face knowing she finally won.

"Yesterday, I found out Christian wasn't my son," I said. "I couldn't have known in a million years all this prior drama had occurred."

"Well, I surely, did," Nicole said. "I actually knew about it for years."

"Why did you stay with your husband, for so long, Nicole?"

"Because that's what a strong black woman does."

"There's one other thing that peaked my curiosity."

"What's that, Damien?"

"Did you have anything to do with Coca-Cola laying me off and the Feds investigating me?"

"Baby, I had to wipe my hands clean from you some sort of way."

"We're officially done here, Nicole. I don't ever want to see you again."

"Don't worry, Damien, my work here has been completed."

I stood up with a disgusted look on my face. Then I grabbed my portfolio and headed for the valet. Meanwhile, Bret finally had enough nerves to approach Nicole after I left.

"Mrs. Jones is everything okay?" he asked. "I noticed things seemed to get quite loud at one point over here."

"Yes, Bret, everything is just fine," she replied. "I just had to get one big gorilla off my back today. Now, bring me a bottle of your finest champagne so I can calm my nerves."

CHAPTER 21

All of that drama lasted almost two hours and now I was traveling on I-285 headed westbound. The last place I wanted to go was home plus I need to clear my head. I still was dazed how Diamond bamboozled me after all these years. More importantly, I was stunned and wondered how Christian would take it once he found out the truth. Now, I could bounce back as I've had my share of storms in life. But I really didn't think he was going to be so fortunate.

"Damn you, Diamond, what on earth possessed you to do something like this?" I asked myself out loud. Then I clinched my right fist and struck it against the steering wheel in anger. "You were nothing but totally selfish from the first day I met you."

I continued to travel on the interstate until the traffic began to slow down. Eventually, my car was moving at a snail's pace and the Atlanta rush hour traffic was in full swing. My cell phone was constantly ringing. It was Diamond calling to give me some half-ass explanation I assumed. I didn't want to listen to what she had to say so I sent all the calls to voicemail.

The only person I wanted to talk to now was Crystal. I at least needed to let her know the deal wasn't finalized. I didn't think I could bring myself to actually tell her what really happened. Eventually, my fingers began to dial her cell phone's number. Without any surprise, she answered pretty quickly.

"Congratulations are in order, Damien," she said answering the phone.

"Hey, Crystal, I need to say something first," I responded.

"Oh no you don't. You're not going to downplay this big day."

"Wait a minute, Crystal, I…"

"It's been two hours since we last spoke and I know you sealed the deal. That means we're going to celebrate. So where are you?"

"I'm stuck in traffic on I-285."

"Where exactly on I-285 are you, Damien?"

"Near the Roswell Road exit headed westbound."

"That's great to hear. You should arrive at my house within the next forty-five minutes."

"Crystal, I think you really need to hear me out first."

"Damien, I've planned something special for us to celebrate your accomplishment. Now, I don't want to hear why we shouldn't. Plus I left the office early as well."

"It's obvious I need to tell you this in person anyway. I'll see you shortly."

"Okay, baby, I'll see you in a little while. Hey, there's one other thing I need to tell you."

"Yeah, what's that, Crystal?"

"No matter what, I'm still proud of you."

"Thanks Crystal I needed that. I'll see you soon."

After I disconnected the call with Crystal, I thought how it was probably better if I told her what happened in person. Besides, she wouldn't even allow me to give her a hint of the mishap.

One hour had elapsed, in the gridlock Atlanta traffic, when I finally made it to the Cascade Road exit. I turned right off the exit and traveled for a mile or two before turning off on another road. Shortly, I had made my way into Crystal's well-kept community. As I drove slowly, I noticed the well-manicured lawns and houses that were worth at least half-a-million dollars. Easily, I found Crystal's house with her white Mercedes S550 parked outside the garage. I pulled into the driveway next to her vehicle. Then I exited my car, walked up the front door, and rang the doorbell.

"Damien, I'm so glad you could make it," said Crystal as she opened the door. She hugged me around my neck before I could barely get through the front door. "Come on in and let's sit down in the living room."

"Okay," I calmly said.

While Crystal closed the front door, I noticed how gorgeous she looked. She had ditched her normal physician attire and was wearing a Victoria Secret outfit. It was sexier than the last one she had on when I was here previously. She was barefoot and grabbed my hand leading the way. I watched her ass shake along with her sexy walk. When we made it to the living room, lit candles were everywhere. Soft jazz music was playing on the stereo system as we took a seat on the sofa.

"Now, just wait right here," Crystal suggested. "I have to get your surprise for you."

"Crystal, that's not important right now," I said.

"Sit down with me for a second because I need to tell you something."

"Damien, I won't sit down until I return with your surprise."

"Fine, Crystal, have it your way. I'll wait here patiently for my surprise."

Crystal hurried off to an adjacent room. There, she retrieved a medium-sized box that was gift wrapped. She walked back into the living room, with a bright smile, and sat next to me.

"This is for you, Damien," she said placing the box on my lap. "It's your surprise."

"What is it, Crystal?" I asked.

"Silly, you have to open it to find out," she said.

I did just that as I tore the wrapping paper off the box. I was amazed, yet surprised, at what I saw. Then I paused for a moment before saying something.

"Baby, it's a new laptop and an expensive one at that," I said. "It has a cool feature where the monitor detaches and can be used as a tablet. Thank you so much."

"Do you like it?"

"I love it."

"I figured you would, Damien. It's going to be perfect for your upcoming client meetings. Plus, you can break it in with the new account you just secured."

"I'm glad you brought that up because I really need to tell you something, Crystal."

"Give me one minute while I grab another surprise for you."

"You promise you're going to let me talk when you get back?"

"Yes, I promise, Damien."

This time Crystal rushed off into the kitchen. While she did, I placed my new laptop on the side of the sofa out of the way. When she returned, she held two glass flutes and a chilled bottle of champagne.

"Now, first things first," she said handing the bottle to me. "Why don't you open this up so we can make a toast?"

"I didn't get the account, Crystal," I quickly said without reaching for the bottle.

"What do you mean you didn't get the account?"

"Put the bottle and glasses down on the cocktail table. Then come and sit next to me. I'm going to tell you a convoluted story that's going to take a while."

Crystal looked withdrawn but she did exactly what I asked. Then I started from the beginning when I first met Diamond and Nicole. Finally, I ended the story by telling her what happened at the restaurant. When I was finished talking, Crystal sat there just shocked.

"Damien, I'm still trying to wrap my head around what you just told me," Crystal announced. "I don't even think Frederick Germaine could have written something like that."

"Who the hell is Frederick Germaine?" I asked.

"Oh, baby, he's an author who writes romantic thrillers. I just so happen to be reading his latest novel called *Lovers*."

"Well, maybe you should tell him my story and how I was played. It probably would hit the best-sellers list."

"Damien, like I told you earlier, I'm still proud of you," said Crystal as she moved closer to me. Then she hugged my upper torso while laying her head on my chest. "Maybe all of this is simply my fault."

"What do you mean?" I asked.

"If that incident didn't ever occur, more than fifteen years ago, at USC none of this would have happened. We both would still be living in Los Angeles. Damien, can you ever forgive me?"

"Crystal, I already forgave you a long time ago. But now, I'm willing to forget about the past so we can both move forward together." Crystal lifted her head off my chest then she looked aimlessly into my eyes.

"Damien, do you really mean that?"

"Yes, baby, I really do."

"I love you, Damien."

"And I never really stop loving you, Crystal."

Our lips met and then our tongues. It had been so long since that happened but it still felt superb. Then my tongue found its way to her breasts and clit. After a while, there was nothing but great love making on the sofa. When round one was over, I popped opened the bottle of champagne. We toasted to our love lasting forever then continued on to round two, three, and four. By midnight, we both were extremely exhausted. While lying on the sofa, the jazz music continued to play as we quickly fell asleep.

CHAPTER 22

Meanwhile, halfway across the city, Nicole was just getting situated into her home. As she closed the front door behind her, she held onto a bottle of champagne in her other hand. A few feet away her husband, Maurice, was standing there with a noticeable sicken look on his face. He was dressed in a pair of Cliff Huxtable pajamas and had a robe on as well. She couldn't help but notice him as every light was on in the dashing home.

"Where the hell have you been, Nicole?" he angrily asked with his arms folded. "Don't you know it's after midnight?"

"I was out, Maurice," she answered swiftly while standing in the foyer.

"Out where?"

"At Prime Restaurant."

"The one in Buckhead?"

"Yes, Maurice."

"They closed over an hour ago."

"I know that. I was out riding around trying to clear my head before I came home."

"Dammit, Nicole, you're drunk! You could have hurt someone or even yourself."

"Don't worry it won't happen again. It was just a single occurrence."

Nicole was slightly frustrated on how the conversation was turning out with her husband. She really didn't care if he was concerned or the ramifications for her actions. With the champagne bottle in hand, she slowly walked over to the adjacent dining room. There she placed the bottle on the stylish table and began to remove the fine China consisting of plates and glasses from the cabinet. She placed the items neatly on the table next to her champagne bottle.

"What are you doing, Nicole?" asked her husband. He had followed her into the dining room but kept a safe distance from her.

"It's called cleaning house, Maurice," she

proclaimed picking up a glass. "I've always hated this China."

"What are you talking about? That's our wedding gift from my parents. Don't you know how much that entire set must have cost?"

"I really don't care if it cost a million dollars, Maurice. I always hated it just like I hate you now!"

Before Maurice had time to respond to his wife's disturbing comment, she hurled the glass in her hand towards his head. With his quick reflexes, he was able to duck in time as the glass struck the wall behind him and shattered.

"What the fuck is wrong with you, woman!" he shouted at the top of his lungs.

"I hate you!" she shouted back.

And just like before, Nicole hurled another glass at him. He dodged this one also as it shattered, too. Suddenly, Maurice was met with a barrage of expensive China being thrown at him. From glasses to plates he was able to avoid being hit as they disintegrated on the wall behind him. The more he avoided the China the more Nicole became frustrated. She began to throw the China even faster hoping to make contact.

"Nicole, will you stop throwing that China at me so

we can talk?" he asked. "And besides, you're going to wake the neighbors."

"Oh, now you want to talk," she said pausing with a piece of China in her hand. "Hell no and forget our neighbors." She continued throwing the China where she left off.

"What in the world did I do to get you so pissed off?"

"You cheated on me and fathered a child with that whore, Diamond!"

"I did what with whom?"

"Dammit, Maurice, I swear if you utter another lie out your mouth I'll pull my pistol out of my purse and shoot your tired ass dead."

"Okay, baby, I remember now but that was such a long time ago. I never loved her."

Nicole paused from throwing the China at her husband momentarily. Plus, she needed to regain her breath from her strenuous workout. She wanted to look at him while he tried to explain himself. Maurice stood there like a scared little bitch holding his hand up in a defenseless stance. He was also wise to keep a safe distance from his crazy wife.

"You gave her a child even though I begged for one

after all these years."

"Baby, it was a mistake. We had been drinking heavily that night, plus she told me she was on the pill after it happened."

"You dumbass, don't you know all women say that to the man they're trying to trap?"

"I know that now, baby. I'm so sorry I can't change the past."

"Fifteen years, Maurice, that's what I gave you. Through all the ups and downs I was there for you. Even when I found out, I still stood by your side like a good wife should do."

"And I appreciate you through all the years. I just want to make everything right again. Now, baby, please put down the China so we can talk about this."

"Where did we go wrong, Maurice?" Nicole asked with a defeated look. Then she suddenly dropped the fine China from her hand. She kneeled down on the hard-wood floor and began to cry profusely.

Maurice was glad he no longer had to avoid being hit by fine China, but he felt guilty as sin. He knew he was the cause of his wife being distraught and angered. Quickly, he rushed over to her. When he reached her, he kneeled down by her while hugging her tightly.

"Baby, I'm so sorry for hurting you after all these years," he boldly stated. "I promise nothing like this will ever happen again."

"It better not, Maurice," she softly said. "Especially since I just had to clean up your mess."

"Don't worry, Nicole, I'm going to get the best marriage counselor money can buy. We're going to get our relationship back to the way it used to be."

"And I want that wretched whore's salon done away with. No more of your money goes into that establishment. Do you understand, Maurice?"

"Say no more, baby, it's a done deal whatever you want."

"I want you to continue to take care of your son but not her."

"I understand."

"There's one more thing I need to mention to you, Maurice."

"Yes, baby, what is it?"

"If you ever backtrack I swear I'll hire the best divorce lawyer your money can buy. Then I'll take half and everything else. I'll also make sure you'll be paying alimony until you're old and gray."

"You have my word nothing like that will ever

occur again. Baby, I love you."

"I still love you too, Maurice."

Maurice continued to hold his wife in his arms as she wept quietly. The pair had nothing more to say after that. They were now more concerned on getting their marriage back on the right track.

CHAPTER 23

It was Friday and Mookie's event at the Boys and Girls Club was scheduled for this afternoon. Ironically, it was one day after my catastrophic meeting with Nicole and Diamond. I awoke early in the morning and called Mookie bringing him up to date on what happened yesterday. He was apologetic and understanding. Mookie even suggested I could take a rain check on the event but I decided to attend. Even though I still felt stunned, I wasn't going to let him or the kids down today.

The drive to Decatur wasn't too far from my condo in Buckhead. As I traveled closer to my destination, I began to feel better. Knowing I could impact our future leaders of tomorrow really meant something to me. I even wore my navy blue suit so I could make a good impression. Like always, once I'm driving, my cell phone rings. As I picked up the phone, I wasn't surprised who was calling me.

"What's up, Raphael?" I asked smoothly.

"Oh, hell no don't tell me it's true, Damien," he exclaimed.

"What's that?"

"All of these rumors that have been circulating, throughout the salon, since this morning. People are saying Diamond is a fraud and you're not her baby daddy. Is that true, Damien?"

"Yes, Raphael, it's true. She conspired to implement a web of lies from the first time I met her. I guess the only good thing that happened is that it all came out."

"Boi stop! And that wicked bitch didn't even have the nerve to show her face in here today. She left the entire salon a message saying she was feeling ill and under the weather."

"Well, after what recently happened I'm sure part of that is true."

"I swear, Damien, I'm going to snatch her ass baldheaded the next time I see her! She'll think twice about wearing that long blonde weave up in here."

"Raphael, you got to calm down. That's not going to solve anything."

"I'll be damn if I let her make a fool out of my first cousin."

"You and I both know things happen for a reason. So, with that being said, this is the way it's supposed to be. Now, calm down and keep your composure."

"I don't know if I can, Damien."

"Raphael, the best way to hurt Diamond is in her pocketbook."

"What do you mean, Damien?"

"I mean you're the best stylist she has in the salon. You easily generate at least seventy percent of all the sales, and no other stylist can come close to that."

"What are you suggesting?"

"That you move on and start your own salon. You already have a strong and supportive clientele that will follow you."

"Yeah, I see your point, Damien. Actually, I've always wanted to own something that was mine. Plus, I know the right person who can help me out financially with the initial start up costs."

"I'm glad you're seeing this from a business perspective. The last thing I need to be doing is bailing you out of the city jail."

"Damien, your point is well taken."

"Now, promise me you're not going to act out with Diamond."

"Hmmmmmm…."

"C'mon, Raphael, you have to promise me."

"Okay, Damien, you win but I'm going to ask Bishop Eddie Wrong to pray for me. I promise I won't whip that whore's ass. Instead, I'm going to look for a location where I can start my own salon."

"That's good I'll talk with you later, cousin. I'm on my way to the Boys and Girls Club in Decatur. I agreed to be a speaker for Mookie's mentorship event."

"You mean tall and fine Mookie who's built like a NFL linebacker?"

"Yes, Raphael."

"The same Mookie with the clean bald head, bulging muscles, and dark chocolate skin complexion?"

"That's the same one."

"Lawd, he can tackle me any day of the week!"

"I'm hanging up now, Raphael."

"What a minute, Damien, I need to ask you one other thing."

"Shoot."

"I know it's been tough for you dealing with Diamond and all. But, seriously, are you okay?"

"Yeah, cousin, I'm fine. What doesn't kill you just makes you stronger."

"Well, you know blood is always thicker than water. I'm here for you if you need anything."

"Thanks, Raphael, that's good to know. I'll talk with you later."

"Chow."

After speaking with Raphael, I finally arrived at the Boys and Girls Club of Decatur. The event was small but nice. There were about five speakers including myself. Also present was a nice spread of catered food the club had paid for. Everyone, including the kids, really enjoyed everything.

When the event was over, I mingled with the crowd. I was able to network with a few business individuals like myself. I was even surprised when a handful of kids came up to me inquiring on how to become an entrepreneur. In all, the nearly two hours I spent there was well worth it. Mookie took it upon himself to walk me to my car after everything had ended.

"Man, I just want to thank you once again for coming out to my event," said Mookie.

"Bro, you know it's no problem," I stated. "Anytime you need me I'm just a phone call away."

We eventually arrived at my parked car. Then we gave each other our customary and brotherly handshake and hug. We had been doing that since college it was normal now.

"Alright, Damien, I'll see you around," he said.

"There's something I wanted to give you before I leave," I announced to my friend. I reached into my inside suit pocket and withdrew an item. "Here's a check made out to your mentorship program right here at the Boys and Girls Club."

"Aw, Damien, you know I already said you didn't really have to make a donation," he proclaimed.

"I insist, Mookie, please take it," I politely ordered. Then I handed him the check.

"Damien, this is a check for five hundred dollars," he said looking at the piece of paper. "Are you sure you can afford to give this donation?"

"Yes, I can," I said smiling. "It was given to me as a blessing that I almost refused. Now, it can be used to help and bless others."

CHAPTER 24

Almost a month had passed by now and I had just about put the incident behind me. It was Saturday the Fourth of July and Mookie was celebrating his birthday. Like his previous birthday celebrations, he only invited close friends and family. He hired a local deejay known for keeping the party live with classic '70's and '80's old school music. His uncle was responsible for manning the food on the grill. This included barbeque chicken and ribs, sausage brats, gourmet burgers, and hot dogs. His mother made sure everything else like collard greens, potato salad, candy yams, plus macaroni and cheese was prepared to perfection.

I had invited Crystal to come along with me. Even

though I talked his ear off about Crystal, Mookie was excited about meeting her. While en route to Mookie's house, I could tell Crystal was somewhat nervous. She sat in the passenger seat speechless as I continued to drive.

"Hey, I want you to relax, okay," I said to her. "We're going to have a great time today."

"Damien, do you think everyone is going to like me?" she asked.

"Baby, they're going to love you. Why wouldn't they?"

"I don't know. I guess I feel uneasy because I never met any of your friends here in Atlanta."

"Crystal, you meet new patients at your office every day."

"Yes, Damien, but this is much different."

"Well, just think of my friends as new patients. And for the one hundredth time, I want you to relax because everything is going to be fine."

"Okay, Damien, I will."

As we pulled up to Mookie's house, I noticed a long line of cars down the street. Music was playing from the rear of the home. But most importantly, we could smell the sweet aroma of barbeque in the air. We both made our way to the front door where Mrs. Wysinger promptly greeted us.

"Damien, I'm so glad you could make it to my son's birthday celebration," she said. We hugged each other and then she turned her attention to Crystal. "Well, who might this pretty young lady be?"

"Mrs. Wysinger, I would like you to meet Crystal," I announced.

"Crystal, it's so good to meet you," she said. "We've heard nothing but great things about you."

"Thank you, Mrs. Wysinger," Crystal said cracking a smile. "It's a pleasure meeting you as well."

"You're from Los Angeles, too?"

"Yes, ma'am, I am."

"Well, down here in the South we're all about good food, love, and family. Now, come over here and give me a hug, girl."

The two women hugged and I could tell Crystal felt more comfortable now. I'm glad Mrs. Wysinger was an expert at breaking the ice with everyone she met.

"Where's the birthday boy?" I asked.

"He's in the back yard entertaining all the guests," Mrs. Wysinger said. "You can go ahead and join him, Damien. I'm going to take Crystal in the kitchen and introduce her to Mookie's girlfriend, Nadine."

"Okay, I'll see you two later on in the back yard."

There had to be at least fifty people in the huge back yard once I arrived there. I noticed Mookie's uncle on the grill then I waved and smiled at him. The deejay was spinning records as a lot of people were dancing or mingling. Mookie was the first person to approach me out of nowhere.

"Damien, my main man," he shouted as he opened his arms. "Glad you could come out."

"Bro, you know I wasn't going to miss your birthday celebration," I said as we hugged.

"Follow me in the house for a minute because I want to show you something."

"Okay, I'm right behind you."

We both ended up in his old bedroom towards the back of the house. While we walked there, he made sure no one noticed us. Then he closed the bedroom door and removed an item from his pocket. It was a ring box and he quickly opened it.

"Well, what do you think?"

"Whoa, Mookie, that diamond solitaire is nice! It's got to be at least two carats, right?"

"Nah, it's only one carat but it took me almost a year to save for it."

"Regardless, Nadine is going to love it. The

194

diamond definitely has clarity, color, and cut."

"Yeah, I figured if she says 'yes' that will be the best birthday present I ever received."

"What do you mean if, bro? What woman wouldn't say 'yes' to a diamond ring like that and a man like you?"

"Damien, I really appreciate that," he said. "I also want to thank you for always being there for me."

"Man, thank you for being there for me as well," I said and we hugged again.

"Now, when we get back outside, don't say a word. This is supposed to be a surprise. My mom doesn't even know."

"My lips are sealed, Mookie.

Later that evening, when the sun was beginning to set and the party was in full swing, Mookie made the deejay stop the music. I made sure Crystal was standing by my side as I put my arm around her. Everyone looked surprised and wondered what was going on. Mookie grabbed the deejay's cordless microphone and asked Nadine to join him at the center of the crowd. When she did, he said a brief speech about how much he loved her. He also stated no other woman on the planet ever made him feel more complete. She quickly became teary-eyed. Then he removed the ring box from his pocket. Quickly, he dropped to one knee and asked her to marry him. She said 'yes' almost before he could get the proposal out of his mouth good. His mom and the rest of the crowd went into a wild cheer.

"Baby, that's going to be us one day real soon," I said to Crystal over the boisterous crowd.

"Oh, Damien, I hope so," she said. "I can't wait to be your wife."

"I love you, Crystal."

"And I love you too, Damien."

I kissed Crystal right about the same time Mookie was embraced with Nadine. I knew right then and there our love for each other was truly authentic. There was no way anything else was ever going to come between us again.

By the end of the year, a lot of things changed. Depending on who you asked, some of it was good while the rest was bad.

Raphael eventually left Diamond's salon and he took all of his clients with him. He opened up a brand new salon in midtown called Raphael's. Katrina helped him broker the deal with a good real estate attorney. She even gave him a small loan so he could get the salon up and running. He quickly worked it off by being her personal stylist on her many business trips. I guess Katrina, the old cougar, wasn't so bad after all.

Ultimately, I sat down with Christian and told him I wasn't his father. This happened because Crystal and I agreed it was the best thing to do. Plus Diamond didn't have the courage to tell him. He took it pretty well and Maurice was quickly there to shower him with expensive gifts. In the end, Diamond's salon closed down due to lack of funds and business. After a while, she later moved back to Chicago and Nicole had the biggest smile on her face.

Crystal turned out to be a networking genius. She pitched my marketing consulting business to all her physician friends and colleagues. Soon I was inundated with more than enough business to keep me busy for years to come. Marriage was in the works between us but we wanted to take our time before that big leap.

At the end of the day, I had matured and come full circle just like my best friend Mookie. My days of being a foolish ladies' man were now well behind me. The best advice Mookie had ever given me was transplanted in my mind forever. And that was how everyone deserves a second chance in the game of life and love.

The End

Discussion Questions

1. Did Damien and Mookie mature at the end of *Ladies' Man 2*? If so, discuss how.

2. Could you sympathize with Nicole and condone her behavior especially with what her husband, Maurice, put her through?

3. Sometimes it's best not to fix relationships that are broken. Should Damien have given Crystal a second chance after everything that happened between them?

4. Could you predict the ending playing out the way it did in *Ladies' Man 2*?

5. Compare and contrast Diamond and Crystal. Before the end, which woman did you believe Damien was going to choose and why?

6. Who was your favorite character and explain why?

7. What specifically didn't you like about *Ladies' Man 2*?

8. Do you think Katrina really enjoyed the company of Raphael or was she using him to have a connection with Damien?

9. Even though the author never mentioned it, did you realize Crystal selected the tarot card that represented 'the lovers' from Mrs. Baptiste?

10. Did you enjoy the descriptive sex scenes in *Ladies Man* or *Ladies' Man 2* more? Explain why.

11. Who were ultimately the winners and losers in *Ladies' Man 2*?

12. Explain how Damien's grandmother and Coach Frazier were instrumental in his life. Do you think the ending would be different if Damien didn't have these two individuals directing his path while growing up?

13. Do you believe the author did a good job of illustrating and setting up the ending to *Ladies' Man 2*? Explain your answer.

14. Do you think the author should continue with *Ladies' Man 3*? Why or why not?

15. Simply answer the following question with yes or no: In the game of life and love, does everyone deserve a second chance?

ABOUT THE AUTHOR

Frederick Germaine has always been fascinated how writing could be so intriguing. It takes dedication and an imaginable thought process to capture an audience within a good novel. After writing leisurely for years, Frederick Germaine decided to independently publish his works. He created his own publishing company called F. Germaine Publishing.

Frederick Germaine's debut novel titled *Ladies' Man* was released in 2011. *Ladies' Man* is an entertaining love novel written from a male-perspective. His debut novel was well received and favorably reviewed among many avid book readers.

In 2012, Frederick Germaine launched his sophomore novel titled *Eye Candy*. Keeping a love and romance theme, this highly unpredictable romantic thriller excites an audience with unforeseeable suspense.

Not to be outdone by his prior works, Frederick Germaine introduced his third novel titled *Lovers* in 2013. *Lovers* is a forcibly exciting love novel that has the readers guessing who's really loving who.

The subsequent year, in 2014, Frederick Germaine finally released the highly-anticipated sequel *Ladies' Man 2*. As with his previous works, readers were absolutely surprised how this finale played out.

Frederick Germaine's achievements include his novels *Lovers* and *Eye Candy* respectively earning a finalist position in the 'Fiction: African-American' category of the 2013 & 2012 USA Best Book Awards, sponsored by USA Book News. He was also named as a finalist for the coveted 2012 National Black Book Festival Best New Author Award.

Frederick Germaine graduated from Jacksonville State University where he earned a Bachelor's Degree in Business. He currently resides in Atlanta, Georgia.

For additional info please visit: www.frederickgermaine.com

9780692223512